TALES OF THE FURTAKERS

Short Stories By

Tom Eberhard

Tom Eberhard

FIRST EDITION

Copyright 1995, by Tom Eberhard
Library of Congress Catalog Card No: 94-90809
ISBN: 1-56002-543-3

UNIVERSITY EDITIONS, Inc.
59 Oak Lane, Spring Valley
Huntington, West Virginia 25704

Cover and interior art by Kim Nesbit

Dedication

For

My Wife Betty

TABLE OF CONTENTS

TALES OF THE FURTAKERS

Short Stories By

Tom Eberhard

CHAPTER I

THREE LEG[1]

In the cloudy dawn, a slender human form, laden with a heavy pack, bent over strange marks in the snow of Barrett Creek. The figure raised a bit, and still hunched over, bobbed down the draw. Underneath a large clumpy willow, he stopped again, crouched lower, and peered into the snow.

As he studied the tracks before him, his twisted mouth opened in a crazy grin and exposed his tobacco stained teeth.

"Can't be!" he thought. "No way! My eyes must be playing tricks."

He stepped to the far side of the willow where the tracks were sharp and clear. He sucked in a gulp of air. "It's him! Three Leg. I've hooked Old Three Leg!" he whispered. "And they said I'd never do it! Yeh, even the great trapper Wojack swore it couldn't be done! Never could Three Leg be lured into a set. But I drew him in, fair and square, and hooked him hard!"

Holding back a laugh, the pursuer broke into a limping trot along the lurching, crazy track of the three-footed coyote. "Three Leg, how did you like my lure? Irresistible wasn't it? And the trap to the side where you didn't expect it. Didn't you smell it Three Leg? Now to find you!"

The pursuer continued his pressing gait, and soon he was drawn into a grove of small aspen. A fresh, damp breeze cooled his heated face as he slowed to pick out the wild dog's track among the numerous stems. "Aha," he thought, as he examined a circle of churned up snow and leaves. "Three Leg hung up here for a little while. See, the grapple hooked onto that little aspen in the center. But how the devil did he get loose?"

The pursuer squinted at the signs of the turmoil around the small aspen, but could not learn what had gone wrong. "Grapple

---

[1]Published in *Trapline Journal*, July, 1983.

must be fouled in the chain," he thought.

The breeze picked up and now struck him in the face. Circling the dense aspen, he spotted Three Leg's prints on the far side. Again, he trotted with a bobbing gait along the strange trail that was made of two normal prints with toes and pads, the tell-tale hole of a footless peg-leg, and the weird thrashings of steel, chain, and grapple.

On the horizon ahead, the sky darkened, and a new, strong wind moaned in the bare limbs of the aspen. The swift air began to catch snow from the ground and twirl it into the tops of the trees.

With concern, the pursuer looked at the sky and fast moving snow. "Better hurry," he thought, massaging the huge numb scar on his right cheek. "Soon the tracks will be gone. But why didn't Three Leg tangle in these trees?" he asked himself again.

Hard icy pellets now rattled off his leather cap and stung his face as he pushed himself along the softening track into a narrow park. The strong wind began to seep away much of his body heat and he felt a clammy chill penetrate his bones.

He lowered his head to avoid the pummelling of hard snow and to obtain a better view of the fading prints. Even so, he began to lose the tracks of Three Leg. Two times he had to circle to locate the trail as it turned up a steep hill.

As the tracks approached a dense stand of fir, the pursuer lost them in a violent blast of snow. In vain he searched the thicket as the gusty winds and flying snow continued to chill his trembling body. He made another wide loop on the high side of the thicket, but could see nothing in the wild, white storm.

"Gone," he thought. "Never find him now. But how did he slip through this thicket without hanging up? Should have staked the trap instead of using a drag. Too late now."

With fatigue and disappointment sapping his strength, he studied the bending evergreens and whirling white. "Guess I'll hole up under these trees until I can see better," he thought. "Feel tired today."

Against the leeward side of a giant fir, the pursuer squatted and pulled a thick down coat from his pack. He fastened the hood over his brown cap and zipped the front all the way to his chin. Trembling, he settled against the massive trunk. "What kind of poison runs through my veins," he wondered, as he rubbed his aching shoulder and swallowed to quell a nausea mounting in his throat. "Lord, could it be something else from that ton of rock that crushed me in '73?"

The puffy coat slowed the loss of heat from his body and he relaxed somewhat. The heavy pulse in his throat, however, continued its uncomfortable pounding, and he shifted with uneasiness.

"Where are you, Three Leg? You rascal, you. For five years,

I've followed your track, trying to lure you into a set. And today I finally hooked you and was about to show everyone that I outsmarted you. You, the wariest coyote in Colorado!

"Now, you may be Two Leg, for you might lose a second foot. But that won't bother you any. You will still run like the wind, kill viciously, and torment man until you die.

"But perhaps I'll hook you again, Three Leg, lure you into another deadly set you can't resist. Track you down, crush your chest and slip off your thick pelt. Then I may be able to say to everyone, even Wojack, that I caught Three Leg absolutely the smartest wild dog of them all."

As he squinted into the flat white of the storm, he wondered who'd be crazy enough to chase coyotes in weather like this. His misshapened face softened as he grinned. "Only a trapper. No one else would enjoy its beauty, its power."

As the wind continued its erratic blasts, the pursuer pondered over the superior cunning of the wild dog. "Hard to catch, these canines that race and kill in the dark. Smart, suspicious, trap shy. Look how long it took me to catch my first one. Me, born and raised on the streets of Chicago. Years. Thought I'd never learn why they circled my sets and dug out the traps. They made mucking out coal seem a snap."

The pursuer shifted his weight onto a hard knee of the fir's trunk to ease the growing discomfort in his shoulder. "The dog's power and endurance are immense," he thought. "They never give up. Even at life's last breath, their hearts pound like a maul and their bodies quiver with hope ready to spring up and bound away should a burst of oxygen shoot through their veins.

"Even so, the dog, with his nose, speed, and suspicion, has the advantage. That is, if you play it right. No trail sets. Has to be a lure set, where he doesn't have to go in. Only if he likes it."

The pursuer shifted again, massaging his shoulder with heavy scarred fingers and staring at the whirling snow. "If I just had one speck of his strength, I'd be a new man."

A wild, frenzied blast of wind and white tore at the huddled figure and unsteadied his perch on the knee of the great trunk. Regaining his balance, the trapper smiled to himself as he thought of the coyote's future. "He'll survive man, no question. And long after I'm gone, the coyote will romp by my grave, squirting on the headstone to mark his territories."

The sky lightened and the snow diminished. The wind, however, swept through the evergreens, whipping their dark green branches and lifting the soft white ice into fast moving devils and puffs. A patch of blue sky bared itself between the swift, gliding clouds.

The pursuer, stiff and still tired, rose to assess the change in the storm. "Better move on," he thought. "Have to be at Somerset by seven for the union go-round. Go down Barrett

Creek to the county road near the giant rock slide. Then follow the road to home."

The wind again took his body warmth, but his walking soon generated enough heat to ward off a chill. Although he knew better, he searched the snow for some sign of Three Leg. The white mantle, however, revealed no sign of the loping dog.

As he entered the willows in Barrett Creek, the force of the wind diminished. The pursuer felt no pressure now, and slowed his pace, plodding with ease through the narrowing canyon. "Hate to lose Three Leg," he thought. "If the storm had only held off another hour."

As the canyon widened near the huge talus slope, the pursuer reached the old Barrett drift fence. Pressing on the top wire, he stepped over the aging barrier. Amidst the squeaking of the wire, he thought he heard a clinking sound in the wind. "Just the fence," he thought. But he paused to listen again.

Hearing only the dull roaring of the wind, he eased down the trail, stepping without crunching the snow, breathing through his open mouth, and listening with his entire body. The wind eased for a moment and he felt a little tingle run down his neck as another faint clinking reached his ears. "Steel chain! Maybe! Just maybe old Three Leg is hung up somewhere close!"

The pursuer stopped, motionless as stone, in a fresh gust of wind. As it quieted, he detected another jingling of chain in the rock field above. His heart thumped like a hammer and his eyes pierced the talus like giant needles as he listened for the direction of the strange sound.

In the large deep rocks near the end of the fence, he spotted something moving. Then he saw a gray tail flick above the wire, and, a second later, a sharp muzzle and two upright ears. "That's him! Three Leg!" he whispered. "Tangled in the fence!"

The pursuer scrambled up the treacherous rocks, slipping between some and barking his shins on the rough edges. As he closed in on the dog, he paused to get his breath and ease a new wave of nausea. Resting on one knee, he opened and closed his left hand to relieve a numbness in his forearm.

As some of his breath returned, he reached over his back and withdrew a stout wooden stick from his pack. He stepped closer to the dancing coyote and worked his feet into the cracks for secure footing.

Sneering at his pursuer, the dog showed his worn, broken teeth that, with his white muzzle, gave away his age. His dull, patchy fur also revealed a pathetic sickness that was riddling his body.

"Three Leg!" the pursuer said, his pulse still thumping hard in his throat. "You're a mess! Why, look at your fur! And your tail! You got the mange! Who would want your worthless hide?"

Even so, the old coyote was not finished. He thrashed among

10

the rocks, back and forth, up and down, pulling with tremendous strength against the number three trap that closed on only one of the toes of his whole front foot.

The pursuer studied the coyote again as it ceased its violent jumping and cowered close to the rocks.

"Three Leg," he whispered. "You poor devil. I know you're hurting bad from the mange. And you will die a slow miserable death."

He bent over the aged dog. "But did I fool you, Three Leg, because you're old and sick? Can't you smell the steel under the dirt anymore? Is that it, old dog?"

He straightened and examined for a moment the vast expanse of the slide. His gaze returned to the old canine, for now it lurched in frenzied desperation to shake the unyielding trap. After a few moments, the coyote quieted and the pursuer bent again, whispering, "But it's better that I kill you, Three Leg, than let you die so wretchedly."

He gripped the stick with both hands, raising it high and into the wind. For a second, he hesitated, wincing from a bolt of new pain in his chest. Recovering, he swung the staff with deadly speed.

The club swept low and missed the dog's head. It struck, instead, the coyote's taut front leg just above the trap, tearing it loose from the jaws. The graying animal shot from the trap in a violent ball of snow and fur. In a flash, he was on his feet, scratching and bounding over the snowy rocks.

Standing bent and quiet, the pursuer watched the coyote fade into the trees above the slide. With a quivering arm, he reached for his cap that had fallen when he had swung at the dog. His sparse white hair flicked in the wind and looked strange against his wrinkled, colorless face.

"Go, Three Leg. Enjoy your last days. You and me, we don't have many left."

CHAPTER II

STUMPTAIL[1]

Now Stumptail wasn't no ordinary coon. He was probably the ornriest ringtail in Franklin County. And the smartest. You see, he was raised on chickens. Mrs. Suffin's white leghorns. So he learned some fancy tastes early. Plus he figgered out cookie jars, garbage cans, and sweet stuff in the garden.

Trouble was, Stumpy got raised as a pet of them spoiled rotten Suffin girls. They brought him up from a tiny baby to a full grown coon. Course they wasn't trappers. Laws no! They was house bred, and about the only thing they could ketch was a cold or sore throat when they wanted to duck school.

So Stumpy got away with murder, tearin' up the house, rippin' the garden, and killin' white leghorn chickens. And the girls thought it was cute. One thing he didn't get away with, though, was his tail. He lost it in a fracas with the lawn mower when he was little. Later on, Mrs. Suffin was wishin' it had been his head.

By fall, Stumpy had got so ornery and raisin' such a ruckus that Mrs. Suffin blew her lid and lowered the boom. Now she wanted to hang the varmint, but on account of the wailin' of the daughters, she relented and dumped Stumpy out ten miles east of here. Real easy then. But a heap of trouble later on.

Now the coon took to the wild purty good, learnin' to ketch crawdads and frogs, and rememberin' how to raid gardens and chicken coops. So from eatin' so good, he grew into one fat coon.

Some of the folks he stole from got real irate and tried to ketch the marauder. Even used dogs. Oh, yeah, they got some snapped traps and pinches of hair, and lots of bayin' from the hounds. But no solid coon. Them close calls just made Stumpy real shy of dogs and steel, and a heap smarter than any run-of-

---

[1]Published in *The Trapper*, December, 1985.

the-mill coon.

For several years, the coon thieved off and on, and up and down Mill Creek. Early in the coon's third fall, a rovin' farm hand got word that the pest was devlin' Ivan Taska real bad. So he stopped at the old farmer's place and asked for a shot at Stumpy, claimin' that he could ketch anythin' that had four legs and hair.

Now silver-haired Ivan ordinarily didn't want no strangers messin' on his place. But he was agin' some and smartin' from the ravages of the tail-less coon. So he gave in.

This here whiz-bang trapper laid out some high falutin' sets with extra smelly lure and bait, all the way from Ivan's hen house to Mill Creek. First thing he nailed, though, was a skunk under the chicken coop, and that didn't set too good with Ivan. Nor the Missus. Then he latched onto one of Ivan's cats on some fancy fish lure. The cat squalled purty loud and Mrs. Taska took it real personal. And when he caught one of Ivan's pet mallards at the spring house, he got run off fast. Real fast.

Although old Ivan hadn't trapped for years, he was feelin' desperate, and figgered he'd have to get rid of Stumpy himself. Diggin' through his tool shed, he fished out some old longsprings and set 'em along Mill Creek. There he made some bank hole sets, shiny crawdads in the water sets, hollow log sets, some with lure and some with bait.

But as fall wore on, he grumbled more and more at his empty traps. Seein' some large tracks near the spring house, he moved a couple of sets close to the fresh sign.

But the tracks just went on by like the sets wasn't even there. Ivan cussed and cussed, 'cause in years past he had never seen a coon that wouldn't try his special smoked fish.

In late December, after more snubs and the freeze-up had set in, Ivan gathered his traps. As he was liftin' his last set, he seen a small boy on the far side of the creek.

"Hmph," Ivan thought. "Must be a rat trapper. But what's he doin' here anyway?"

Now the boy seen Ivan right off, and tried to wave while he drug a gunny sack along the frozen bank.

Not feelin' real friendly, Ivan snorted as the boy slid across the ice with his sack.

"Whatta you want, boy?"

"Oh, nuthin', Mistah Taska. I jes got somepin' to show you."

Ivan frowned real mean at the sack. "Rats? Or you got some of my ducks?"

"No, suh. Coon. And he ain't got no tail."

Ivan's lower lip was quiverin'. "Don't lie to me, boy. Lemme see that sack."

Shakin' now like a palzied house dog, Ivan dumped a big, tail-less coon onto the ice. He stared at the ringtail, then at the

14

boy.

"Stumptail! How'd you get 'im? Found 'im killed along the road?"

The boy was afraid some and spoke low. "No, suh. Ketched 'im by 'is front foot. See?"

Ivan glared as he fingered the front foot. "What on?"

The boy showed his teeth in a skimpy grin. "Bes' coon bait goin'."

By now, Ivan's voice was squeaky and high pitched. "What bait, boy?"

"Chicken. White leg'ern."

CHAPTER III

MADAME AND THE SKUNK

On the classy side of Fayette, Madame LeMay was spiffing up her yard for a fall garden bash. Standing on the patio of the spreading ranch home, the towering matron snapped at the gardener in language she used only on her servants.

"Sanders, that skunk's gotta go! The smell's gettin' to me. You get ridda him before Saturday, or I'll have your hide on the wall!"

Her dark eyes bored into the aging caretaker. "And no stink. No smell anywhere! D'ya hear?"

George bent over the edge of the patio and examined the fresh burrow. "Yes'm. I'll get 'im. He's as good as gone."

Noticing a large black poodle that lay in the shade of a large azalea, he rose and said, "But it would help, Mum, if you would please keep Cheree inside every morning 'til seven, so's she wouldn't tangle with the skunk. If'n he's in the trap. Just the next couple of days."

Madame lit a long cigarette that hung from her gold trimmed ivory holder, and exhaled a thin stream of smoke through heavily painted lips. "Alright. I'll see that she stays in, but you get that skunk."

After supper that evening, Old George gathered a live box trap, a fish head, and some scent, and returned to the patio. "Ain't no skunk alive that'll pass up this lure," he reasoned, as he placed the attractants inside. "Now I'll put it right next to the hole. Then set this wobbly treadle. There."

Standing, his face beamed with confidence. "That pesky skunk is as good as caught," he muttered. "Just drown 'im in the goldfish pond. No stink." Smiling to himself, the old man shuffled home in the quiet evening air.

Rising early, the caretaker hurried to the LeMay gardens in the damp mist of dawn. Nearing the wire trap, he caught his breath. "Oh, oh, somethin' dark in there. Aha. Got 'im. Nothin'

17

to it." Stepping nearer the trap, he bent to make sure. "Rats, a dadburned cat! Wouldn't that frost yer whatever!"

He opened the trap door and hissed at the feline. "Scat! Get outa here!"

The cat flew from the trap and shot across the green velvety lawn, disappearing into the bordering shrubs.

Muttering, George picked up the trap with its potent smelling bait and hung it on the far side of the garage. "Better keep it outside," he thought. "Madame wouldn't want those fumes floating into her Mercedes."

That evening, George reset the trap at the burrow entrance, but failed to catch the skunk. Through the next three nights, he set the trap again, but missed the black and white pest each time.

"Better get 'im soon," he thought, his ruddy face puzzled from his failure to nab the varmint. "Only two days left and Madame's getting real antsy."

He shoved a large gob of tobacco into his mouth. "Well, I gotta do it. Set a leghold trap in that hole and tie it to a long wire. Then drag 'im real slow into the goldfish pond and drown 'im. From that mulberry bush where he won't see me."

At sundown, Old George set his number two trap in the mouth of the skunk's den. "That'll hook 'im for sure," he reasoned, as he smoothed dirt over the trap and laid some sticks for stepping guides. "Now to run the wire to the bush."

As he rechecked his set, Madame and two visiting dames slid onto the patio. Madame's tight fitting black and white gown rustled as she walked. "Geoahge, my deah, I do trust you will tidy up the yard this evening?"

"Uh, oh, Fang's impressin' some high rollers tonight," he thought. "Yes'm. I'll finish by tomorrow."

"Wondahful, Geoahge, wondahful."

Tipping his railroad cap, the chunky gardener plodded toward the front drive and made his way home. "Hope she remembers to keep the dog in tomorrow," he thought, rubbing his chin.

The following morning, George arose late and hurried out the back door. "Gotta check that trap, no time to eat." Reaching Madame's patio, he sneaked to the mulberry bush and pulled on the wire.

"Oh, yeah. Got 'im this time. Sure hope he doesn't squirt 'fore I get 'im to the pond. But how is he caught? All four feet look free! Is he hung by a pinch of skin? Better go slow so he doesn't pull out."

George eased the skunk into the open and, keeping hidden, dragged the animal toward the pond. Watching over the tops of his glasses, his intense expression turned into bewilderment as a screen door banged. His eyes caught a bounding black form streaking through the yard.

"Laws! The mutt's loose! Gotta drown the skunk quick!"
George rose, and with trembling hands yanked on the wire.
His shouts turned into high pitched screams as the dog veered
toward the pond. "Get away! Cheree! Get away! You clumsy
mutt! No! No!" Spotting the tail-raised skunk, Cheree bored into the animal
and shook it with fast snapping jaws. Essence shot into the air
and the poodle retreated, sneezing and sliding her face in the
grass. She paid little attention to the mauled skunk as it rolled
free of the trap and staggered into the nearby azaleas.
Fumes filled the garden, rising from the rocks, lawn, and
poodle. At the patio door, Goldie Brown, the squat cook,
watched with bulging eyes.
Old George trembled with despair. "Whoever let the mutt
out? Fang's gonna be wild! What a mess!
"Well, better take the mutt home. At least I can wash him
with skunk-off. But the garden! It's gonna stink for days!
"C'm'ere Cheree! Quit running off! Gad, how'm 1 gonna
catch this mutt? She's wild! If she runs into the house stinkin',
I'm done fer.
"Need a leash," George mumbled, shaking as he hurried into
the entry way. "Yeah, there's one. Hey, Goldie, get me a piece
of meat so's I can catch the mutt."
Goldie frowned as she looked into the refrigerator. "Hell,
George, what are you gonna do when you catch the mutt? Ain't
nuthin' that will take off skunk. You'll just get stunk up
yourself. Fun Huh? Madame's gonna love you. Here, try this left
over sausage."
Grabbing the tidbit, George hurried into the yard. "Alot she
knows. Dumb woman. Skunk-off gets it off."
Spotting the restless dog, George whistled. "Here, Cheree.
Look. Sausage."
The dog approached with her head extended, nose quivering.
Seeing George's trembling hand reach for her neck, she bolted,
raced around the gold fish pond, and rolled in the grass.
George gritted his teeth. "I'll get you, mutt, if it takes all
day. Gotta get me a rope. Then lasso the crazy hound."
Retrieving a small rope from the garage, George fashioned a
loop on one end. "I'll make her reach through the loop to get the
bait. Then she's mine."
After several more crazy runs around the yard the dog
slowed and tiptoed toward George and the bait. With her head
held high, she reached through the loop and mouthed the
sausage.
George jerked the rope and tightened the snare. "Ha!
Gotcha! Fight all you want, but you're goin' to my place and get
ridda the stink."
At home, George finished drying the poodle with a large

19

worn towel. "There, mutt, you smell better, only a trace of skunk left. But I've gotta find more skunk-off and spray the garden."

Begging the last bottle of essence remover from a young trapping companion, George returned to the garden, mixed a solution of the skunk-off, and sprayed the area of battle.

Goldie walked onto the patio, her white cook's uniform stretched drum tight across her broad form. " 'Fore she left this morning, Madame said for you to put out the tables early tomorrow." She hesitated as a nasty grin exposed her gold tooth. "That is, if you're still alive."

George set his jaw and glowered at the cook. "Wonder if Fats let the mutt out," he thought. "Wouldn't put it past her. Well, I'd better put out the tables today. Might be fired tomorrow."

After placing the furniture, George plugged the burrow and studied the situation. "Still smells. I'll never be able to explain this. 'Bout like arguin' with a slobbered-up bull dog. Although I do remember one time when she was human. Givin' me this job when I was down and out."

The following morning, George stayed home, unwilling to face the Madame's wrath. His grizzled face relaxed as he observed a light drizzle falling in the yard. "Well, the party'll have to move inside. Maybe the smell won't be so bad in there with all the French perfume."

As he prepared to wash his breakfast dishes, he responded to a rap at the door.

"Yeah, Fats. What's up?"

The heavy cook wiped some rain from her nose. "Madame's upset."

"Yeah, the stink."

"Yeah, the stink. But she's mad, too, because you didn't show up this morning. She's needin' help to move the tables inside on account of the rain. As for the smell, you're gonna have to explain that."

George snorted and punched a gob of leaf tobacco in his cheek. "Guess I'd better go. Can you give me a lift?"

Reaching the spreading ranch style home, George followed Goldie into the kitchen. Inside, he hesitated, melting from Madame's piercing glare. "Mornin', Mum. Nice mornin'."

"Nice morning, hell! These tables are drenched and I want 'em inside! Quick! And what about the stink? I told you no stink. And you smell up the whole yard!"

George raised his eyes to meet hers. "Well, Mum, you see, the poodle pushed open the screen door and tangled with the skunk before I could drown 'im. The door wasn't latched."

In an uneasy silence, George and Goldie stood still as stone, meeting Madame's eyes with theirs and moving not a quiver.

Madame turned and gazed in the patio, standing with her arms folded on her bosom. "Door not latched?" she thought. "Oh, Lord, did I leave it open when I went to town?" Again she examined her servants' faces in the awkward silence. Again she found them unwavering and mute. The lips on her stern face tightened, her eyes narrowed. "Well, you two, get these tables inside and dry 'em off. And set 'em up. We've got work to do."

Moving onto the patio, Goldie walked close to George. She held her head down as she whispered in a hoarse, raspy voice. "Man, you sure got outa that scrape easy. You never lost a hair. How come you're so lucky?"

George bent over to grab one end of a heavy table. "Not all luck, Fats. Smarts. Just plain smarts. Ain't all us old trappers smart?"

CHAPTER IV

CRAZY HENRY[1]

In the piercing cold of pre-dawn, Eric Sloan and his heavy burden broke through the ice of the great pond on Alamosa Creek. Gasping and sputtering, the sixteen-year-old flailed at the sliding chunks of ice, trying to keep afloat. "Where is the shore?" he screamed to himself, as his frantic lunging broke new slabs from the edge. "Oh, god, how will I ever get to the bank?" he cried, half choking from shock and fear. "Gotta find the bottom," he hissed. "Go down, legs!" he shrieked, as his feet touched the muck. Orienting himself with the sliver of moon above, he churned toward the north edge of the large pond, tearing at the ice with numb hands. "There, made it!" he cried as he climbed onto solid ice near the bank. "Oh, why did I ever cross this crazy pond? And my bobcat! He's in there! What will I do? Can't go in after him. I'll die!"

Gaping at the aftermath of broken ice, he felt the dread of intense cold gripping his soaked head, limbs and body. "Gotta get outa here! Get moving! Pickup's a long way. Have to make it or freeze!"

With his outer garments and pack now stiffening, he trotted through six inches of loose snow and onto his old trail, his soaked boots sloshing and turning colder with each step. He shoved his numbed hands against the skin of his belly as he stomped along the snowy path. "Oh, they hurt!" he cried as he neared the rim of Alamosa Canyon. "But gotta keep movin'. I'll freeze if I stop!"

Although the ridge top was easier terrain, Eric's pace dragged and he assessed his situation. "Dunno if I can make the pickup. Feet are getting numb. Hands numb, cold all over. Gotta get warm quick!"

---

[1]Published in *The Trapper*, February 1986.

As the eastern sky brightened, the youth spotted a familiar landmark. "Crazy Henry's sheep camp! Maybe I can make that!" And his pace quickened from the new hope. "Have to make a fire there," he reasoned. "Pour in lots of cheater. But how can I strike a match? My hands feel like stones!" Plodding toward the cabin, he felt as though he were walking on footless stubs. "Where is that shack, anyway," he wondered, as his reasoning blurred. "It's gotta be here somewhere."

In the dim light, he perceived the dim outline of the shack. Stumbling through an open gate, he struggled toward the sagging cabin. "Hope it's open," he muttered, shuffling up the porch and shaking the rickety door.

"What a racket! Dogs! Crazy Henry must be here! I sure hope he's sober enough to control those mutts." Shaking, he stepped closer to the door and rattled it again.

The ruckus increased at the second rap, and Eric backed from the entrance. Amid the yapping, however, the youth thought he heard a different noise.

"Basta, perros, basta!"

In the new silence, Eric heard the latch lift and the door opened a crack. Crazy Henry's bloodshot eyes peered through the slit.

"What the hell d'ya want? And what're you doin' here this time a day?"

With his thoughts muddled and slow, Eric stared at the haggard, wavering man. "Lost my cat in the pond. Fell in. Cold. God, I'm cold. Can I get warm, please?"

Henry opened the door. "Fell in? What for? Ain't you got a brain?" He fell into a fit of coughing that bent him to his knees.

Rising, he spat on the porch and whispered. "Well, get in, Gringo. Back of the stove. I'll fire it up. C'mon, dogs won't bother." Again he coughed, a tight hack that hissed and cracked.

Clad in sagging long underwear, Henry staggered to the stove and shoved some wood into the fire box. Stooping, he grabbed an enameled can and slopped some kerosene into the opening.

The petrol ignited on impact, shaking the stove and shooting flames close to Henry's hairy face. "Son of a bitch!" he screamed, backing away from the heat and trying to slide the lid over the blazing hole.

As the fire subsided, the sheepman recovered and he stared at the jerking, lethargic boy. "You been trappin, kid?"

Eric struggled to reply. "Yeah. I'm Eric Sloan. But can you help me take off these clothes? Can't move my hands. Numb. Feet, too."

Hesitating, Henry stroked his wrinkled chin, then fingered Eric's frozen garments. "Jesus, kid, you're in bad shape," and he pulled at the stubborn garments. Finishing, he dragged a heavy comforter from his bed. "Here, wrap in this. But keep your ears away from the stove. They look frost bit."

With unsteady hands, he filled a heavy white cup with rust colored coffee. "Here, drink this."

Eric stared at the cup. "Can't. Hands won't work."

"Jesus, kid. Here, I'll hold it."

With uncoordinated hands, Henry tipped the cup at the boy's mouth and slopped a good portion down his chin. He continued to pour in more, and in a short time, the boy's violent shivering eased.

"You gonna help me get my cat? It's a big tom, worth at least $300."

Henry frowned at the redheaded boy. "Ain't never seen a $300 cat." He lit a cigarette and hung it on his lower lip. "In a pond, huh? Where's it at?"

"About a mile upstream. It's that big beaver dam near McIntyre sheep trail."

The sheepman turned his head, and, reaching under the bed, he lifted a large bottle of tokay. He swallowed several large drafts, cleared his throat, and spat in the wood box.

"Tell you how I can get that cat, kid," he said, gulping more wine and speaking in a low, hoarse voice. "After the sun's up, take my horse and bust the ice. Then send that old mutt, Pedro, into the water. He'll drag gato out. Trained him years ago to crawl into beaver houses and bring 'em out."

Trembling, the old man hacked and gagged, then crumpled onto the bed and stared at the ceiling.

Gaping in shock at Henry's behavior, Eric fingered his swollen ear lobes. "Just have to get to that pond," he thought. "By myself, 'cause Henry's out for the day. Guess I can use those boots by the door. C'mon, sun, warm things up."

Three hours later, as the old cabin creaked from the warming of the sun, Eric put on his dried clothes and drank another mug of sour coffee. He limped to the door and checked the boots for size. "They'll do," he thought, and he tucked them under his arm as he eased out the door.

In the brilliant sunlight, Eric grabbed a pole axe from the woodpile and trudged along his earlier tracks. He limped a little from the tender toes and gritted his teeth as the cold stabbed his ears through the knitted cap.

Reaching the pond, the youth studied the edges and the path of broken ice that had refrozen. "Sure looks different in daylight," he thought, pulling on the boots. "No wonder I fell in! There's a spring on the north side. That'll be a good place to start. Shallow. I'd better get a pole."

Grabbing a dead quakie, he waded into the open water and broke ice with the axe. Then he swept the long pole underneath the shelf trying to bump the sunken cat. "Where is he anyway?"

he wondered. "Have to bust more ice. Reach out farther."

He waded as far as the skimpy boots would allow, breaking what ice he could, shoving slabs under the shelf, and sweeping for the cat. Soon his arms turned to rubber and he stepped from the water to rest.

Refreshed, he searched from a different angle but found no cat. Trying from yet another position, he chipped and probed, but had to rest for another time. "Can't do no more," he thought. "Beat. Water's too deep. I'll have to come back Sunday with chest waders and a horse. Then I'll get 'im."

Somewhat rested, the youth rose and strode for Henry's cabin. As he trudged along, a strong, fresh wind struck his back. "Might be a storm coming," he thought, as he pounded up the steps of the cabin and roused the dogs.

"Better tell Henry thanks for the help," he thought, and he peered through the window. "Looks like he's still on the bunk," he whispered. "Better leave the boots and axe outside and head for the ranch."

Arriving home late, Eric was pressed to explain why he had fallen into the pond. His mother was curt. "You'd better use your head. What would you have done if Crazy Henry wasn't there?"

"Don't worry, Mom. I was okay. Guess I'd better get my work done," he said as he hurried out the back door.

After supper that evening, Eric dove into his cold bed, yielding to the exhaustion from the strenuous adventures on the trapline and week-end chores. At dawn, he awoke a little late, and, jumping from his bed, he gaped out the window. "Snow! Must be a foot deep! And still snowing!"

Sinking onto his bunk, he stared at his socks. "Never get the cat now. Snow'll be three feet deep up there. Guess I'll have to write him off. Rats."

Disappointed, Eric spent the following week on horseback, pulling legholds and setting a few snares. "Snag me a cat yet," he thought, tying a loop to hanging brush over some fresh cat tracks. Might even hook a coyote."

The week passed, and on Friday evening, Eric listened to his mother's plea. "Better visit with Crazy Henry. He's sick with pneumonia at the county hospital."

After supper, Eric drove to the hospital to see the ailing sheepman. Walking into his room, the youth stared at the thin, wasted form. "How is it with you, Henry?"

The old man turned and stared at the youth. "Poco," he hissed. "Fulla needles and pills. Who is it?"

"I'm Eric Sloan. I came to thank you for warming me up last Saturday."

Henry's face remained cadaverous, and his voice was weak and raspy. "Oh, yeah. The kid who fell in. Whatever happened? I thought you needed some help to get your cat?"

Eric peered at the tubes in the old man's nose. "Yeah. I couldn't do any good by myself. And I stopped by later, but you were asleep. So I went home. And then it snowed."

Crazy Henry narrowed his cloudy eyes and suppressed a cough. "You quit too soon, Sloan. Went up a horseback, me and Pedro. Busted ice and rolled your cat. And you know, I fell in, too. Horse stumbled. Damn, I was cold. But we got back before dark."

Eric shook his head. "C'mon, now, Henry. Sounds kinda rich, you finding that cat."

The sheepman eased his head against the pillow and exposed his decaying teeth in a thin smile. "No joke, Sloan. Look in my shearin' shed. Your cat's there, lookin' 'bout like you."

"Like me? What do you mean?"

"Like you was when you came to my door. Froze stiff."

CHAPTER V

SMARTER THAN THE FOX[1]

Tim Hansen gasped as he glanced through the kitchen window. "Bus is coming!" Jumping from his chair, the slender boy flew through the back door of the weathered farm house and raced down the lane in the crisp November air. Stomping up the steps of the bus, he puffed and scanned the occupants. "McLane girls!" He shuddered with dismay as he shot to the rear and dove into an empty seat.

"Late! Late! Skunk trapper's always late! Isn't he ever on time? Oh, wait, dummy can't tell time. So how could he be on time?" The high pitched words of the girls rattled through the bus as Tim slumped on the seat and tried not to hear them. "Wish I had a rock, then I'd fix 'em," he whispered to himself.

After school that afternoon, Tim arrived home late, having stopped at the neighbor's farm. Dragging into the kitchen, the sandy haired boy threw his tattered books on the wood box and slid into a chair. "Mom, Mr. Yerkes said I could trap rats on his river land!" His eyes fell as he hesitated. "But he wouldn't tell me nothin' about catchin' fox. Just said you had to be smarter than the fox."

Harriet Hansen studied the disappointment on her son's gaunt face as she pushed a kettle of chicken to the rear of the stove.

"Well, Son, have you asked Mr. McLane? He's trapped for years, even more than Mr. Yerkes."

The small boy hung his head. "Mom, I hate those McLanes. All they do is tease and call me dumb." He stifled a sob as he laid his head and arms on the table.

The worn, graying woman pressed her son's bony shoulder. "Now, Tim, don't be hard on the McLanes. They've been real

---

[1]Published in *Trapline Journal*, August 1984.

good neighbors these past years. Especially since your father died. Tell you what, I'll see George next week and ask him about taking fox."

Through the dry fall, Tim's interest in his trapline held strong, even though his catch had diminished and his mother brought home no tips on catching fox.

By mid-December, Tim had caught a dozen muskrats, and, in some of his sets intended for raccoon, he nailed some of his old adversaries, the skunks. In other coon sets, he caught only bits of hair and skin in his aging number one traps.

Hurrying home from his trapline on the Saturday before Christmas vacation Tim skipped with light feet. "Fur buyer is comin' today," he said to himself. "Maybe Mom will let me buy a couple of fox traps with the money."

The frail boy broke into a trot as he entered the yard and looked for the buyer's pickup. Seeing nothing, he burst into the kitchen, his patched Levis hanging on his hips and a faded jacket flopping with each step. "Did the fur buyer come, Mom?"

Harriet continued pressing clothes. "Yes. He left 28 dollars for the rats and skunks. And guess what else?"

Tim hesitated, his mouth open and head tilted. "What, Mom?"

"He gave me the name of a dealer that sells books on fox trapping."

The youth grinned, showing his half-emerged front teeth. "Real fox trappin' secrets? Honest, Mom? Will you send for it? And help me read it?"

Harriet's tired features were warm but with a flicker of sterness. "I'll show you how to order the book, Tim, but you'll have to read it mostly by yourself."

A touch of doubt erased Tim's wide grin. "And can I buy a couple of fox traps with the fur money?"

"Now, Tim, there's more important things you need than traps, like clothes and Christmas money. That book is about all we can afford now."

Tim looked away as the hollows under his eyes deepened. "Heck, sure need some big traps. But maybe Mom will surprise me and get some anyway," he thought.

A few days before Christmas, Tim recieved a brown envelope in the mail. His eyes were bright as he tore the flap and extracted the booklet. Squinting, he rotated the booklet a half turn to the right and stumbled over the simple words, "Red and Grey Foxes, How to Trap Them." His face was intense as he thumbed through the book and studied the sketches. After several labored trips over the pages, he grasped some of the meanings, and yearned to set for the wiliest of canines. As the last days before the holiday passed, Tim continued to pour over the drawings and set one of his small traps in the dirt. "Boy, sure hard to tell where the trap is at, bein' covered with dirt. Where is the treadle, anyway?"

His hopes of getting some large traps remained high, and early on Christmas morning, he raced into the cold, tiny living room and looked under the tree. All he could see, in addition to the gifts he had placed, were several more presents, some with his name on them. Grasping the boxes, he shook them. "Heck, too light for traps," he reasoned, and he returned them under the tree.

Moments later, Harriet, clad in a faded tan bathrobe, hurried into the living room. "Sometime, Tim, I'm going to beat you to the tree. When did you get up, anyway?"

Tim appeared not to hear. "Can we open now, Mom?"

"Better wait for Grandma. She's on the way."

As the old woman hobbled into the room, Tim sorted the presents. "Here, Mom. These are yours. And here's some for you, Grandma."

He grabbed his two packages and tore off the paper. "Oh, Mom, this is super!" he said, as he slipped into the bright green and gold coat. "It'll really keep me warm on the river."

"Now, just a minute. You're not wearing that good coat trapping!"

"Heck, Mom. I won't wreck it. Honest."

After Harriet and Grandma opened their gifts, Tim remembered his chores and tripped out the back door. He shot down the weakening steps and halted. "What was that on the porch?" he wondered, and he returned to investigate. Kneeling, he examined a cardboard box of rusty objects at the top of the steps. "Fox traps! Two of 'em! But where did they come from? And what's wrapped in this old paper? Scent? Oh, boy! But how did they get here?"

Grasping the number two coil spring traps and bottle, he raced into the house, with the long chains slapping the floor and furniture legs. "Hey, Mom! Look! A couple of fox traps! Did you get 'em for me? Oh, thanks, Mom! These are just what I wanted!"

Harriet frowned at the clutter of rusty metal. "They're not from me, Tim. Where did you find them?"

"On the back porch. Wonder who left them there? Wasn't you, was it, Grandma?"

The old woman limped to the jumble of iron and wrinkled her brow. "Laws, no. Where would I get any old traps?"

"And look, Mom. Scent! Ain't that great?"

Still puzzled, Tim recalled his chores, and laid the traps by the stove. After hurrying through the morning's work, he returned and got one of the traps working. The boy fashioned a stake from a short rusty bolt, and fastened the chain to it with wire. He stuffed the trap into a sack that held his bait and other

31

tools and trotted toward the river, still wondering who had left the traps on the porch. As he neared the winding waterway, a trickle of muskrat blood leaked onto the back of his new coat.

At the river's edge where he had noticed considerable fox sign, he stopped and examined the ground. "Where should I put the trap?" he wondered. "By the dung, that's the best place." He pulled the small book from his pocket and studied the sketch of the dirt hole set. "Gotta dig a place for the trap," he concluded, and, grasping the hatchet, he chopped a bed in the sand. In the center he pounded the stubborn, wobbly stake. "There. Finally got it deep enough."

Referring to the sketch again, he placed gravel over the stake and chain, set the trap, and wiggled it into the loose soil. He covered the treadle with waxed paper and sprinkled the entire trap with fine sand, levelling the soil as he went. "Boy, that looks good, can't tell there's a trap there. Now a hole for the bait."

From his pocket, he withdrew the fox book again and looked at the drawing of the dirt hole. Nine inches from the treadle to the hole. "But how far is nine inches? Well, this oughta be close enough," and he bored a small hole and scattered the dirt. "Now for some smelly bait. Phew, sure stinks," and he dropped a muskrat leg into the hole with some juice. "Now, for some scent." Unscrewing the top of the bottle, he sniffed the scant amount of watery liquid. "Smells like pee. Well, the book says it's the best scent," and he dribbled some on the edge of the hole. "Oh, yeah, have to brush out my tracks and put those fresh droppings by the hole. Boy, that oughta get a fox," he thought, as he smoothed out the sand.

Tim turned and raced for home, for now he craved a Christmas dinner of chicken, rolls and pie. He pounded onto the back porch and through the kitchen door. "Hey, Mom! I made me a fox set and it sure looks good."

Harriet looked at him and scowled. "Tim, I told you not to wear that coat trapping. And look, you've got some blood on it already. You get busy and wash off the gunk right now!"

Tim removed his coat and looked for the blood. "Heck, just a little muskrat juice. Won't hurt nothing," he thought, and he shuffled into the washroom and scrubbed out the stain.

During the rest of Christmas vacation, Tim visited his fox set every morning, but caught nothing and could see no fresh sign. Puzzled, he added more bait and urine to the hole. "Maybe this fresh dropping will help too," he thought, and he placed a scat into the narrow depression.

Through the following week, the countryside remained dry as Tim checked his traps. His hopes of catching the elusive canine dimmed, for he saw no fresh fox sign anywhere near his set. As a fast moving storm blanketed the Hansen farm on

Friday, Tim felt more discouraged. "How will I catch anything now in snow and frozen ground?" he wondered.

On Saturday morning, Harriet surprised Tim with extra work and the boy fretted as he helped repair the sagging hen house in the biting cold. By mid afternoon, however, he finished and shot for the river.

The dipping sun bounced off the snow and struck Tim's eyes with fierce rays as he trudged toward the ice bound stream. Nearing a little rise along the bank where he had made his fox set, Tim stopped. Then he raced ahead with the speed of a rabbit for the set was a disk of brown in the white of the snow.

Reaching the set, he ran his eyes over the torn dirt. "Oh, oh, sure had somethin' here. Everythin' chewed up and messed up!" He bent over the soil as a wave of disappointment smothered his spirit. "But where is the trap?" He dug at the dirt with his hands, first in the center, then around the edge. "Gone. Everythin's gone, stake and all. Whatever happened?" He bit his lower lip as the disappointment swelled.

Looking at the disturbance once more, he noticed some droppings in the dirt. "Was a fox, alright, but where did he go?" Tim examined the surrounding snow. "There's his track, dragging the chain and stake! Heading toward the river!"

The boy trotted after the unusual prints as they turned down the bank and onto the frozen river. There he stopped, for the tracks disappeared on the glassy, windswept ice. Dumbfounded, the boy slid along the ice, searching one patch of snow after another, but finding no sign of the hooked fox.

As dusk deepened, Tim studied the far side of the river with its scattered patches of purple willows and olive gray cottonwoods. "Maybe he's over there," he thought, as he started across the ice. In the middle of the river, he stopped. "Better not, it's McLanes." Biting his lip again, he lowered his head and shuffled home, his worn coat flopping and the cold biting his frail body.

After a seemingly endless hike, Tim stumbled through the rear door and leaned over the kitchen range. His ears stung more than ever, and he tried to warm them with frigid palms, paying no attention to the aroma of fresh bread and simmering beef.

" 'Bout time," Grandma said. "You taken up livin' with the owls?" She limped to the stove and lifted a bowl of steaming beef and noodles. "Better sit down, Tim, and take in these hot vittles. You look froze."

Tim relinquished his niche by the stove and slid to the table on a white bentwood chair. He gazed at the dish without eating, oblivious to the thud of the front door as it closed.

Harriet moved to the warmth of the dimly lit kitchen, her thin face barely hiding a smile. "Tim, where have you been? Someone's been looking for you all afternoon."

Tim appeared not to hear, and hung his head.

Harriet bent over the boy and pressed her cheek against his icy face. "Tim, did you lose a trap with a fox in it? The McLanes were here and said they found a grey fox with a trap on its rear foot tangled in some wire above the river."

Tim popped up, his eyes glistening with tears. "But that's my fox, Mom. It's not theirs!"

Harriet pressed her son's cheek again. "Yes, they thought so. They left it on the front porch."

Tim leaped from the table and ran out the front door. With tears still on his cheeks, he held up the fox by a hind leg. "Oh boy! I caught me a big old grey fox! Ain't he purty? Gotta show Mom."

Returning to the kitchen, Tim lifted the fox above his head. "See, Mom. A real fox. And I caught 'im."

"Yes, Tim, he's a beauty, and I'm pleased that you caught one. But I think you should run over to McLanes and thank them for killing it and bringing it here."

Tim's eyes fell as he stroked the back of the fox. "Yeah, okay, Mom. But would tomorrow be okay? Oughta skin 'im tonight."

"This evening might be better to see Mr. McLane. He said foxes are hard to skin. And maybe he would help you."

Tim looked at his mother, his grandmother, then fixed his gaze on the fox. "Might be okay to go over," he thought. "Then those McLane girls could see that I'm a real fox trapper."

"Yeah, I'll go over. After supper. Better hang him outside now."

As Tim released the fox's foot from the trap, a puzzled frown crept onto his face. "Mom, I wonder how Mr. McLane knew this was my trap?"

Harriet walked to the kitchen window and pretended to adjust the curtain. "Well, Tim, I think Mr. McLane recognized the trap as one of those he gave you."

"Really? For sure, Mom? He's the one who gave me those traps at Christmas?"

The youth stared at the trap, his mouth barely open, waiting for words to come. In the dim light and quiet of the kitchen, he whispered, "Guess I got alot of thankin' to do."

CHAPTER VI

THE VACATION

In the spacious hallway of the Long Island home, Martha Bothwell tried to smooth a crease in her silver gown.

"Why so late, George? Have you forgotten Senator Dorquet's victory ball? It's past six already, and you know how I detest being late."

Noticing George's strained face, she softened her tone.

"You know, your chance for that federal judgeship depends on your being there."

Avoiding his wife's scowl, George hung his narrow-brimmed hat and grey tweed coat in the closet.

"Now, Martha, don't fret. We'll be there in time. How could I forget a banquet for a dork?"

"George!"

"Sorry, I forgot the French flair. Anyway, come Sunday, I'm off to the marsh. Scott is counting on it."

Placing her hands on her hips, the silver-haired matron continued pressuring her husband.

"Honestly, George, how can you be serious about going to that despicable camp? It's disgraceful enough that our son lives there, shooting geese and trapping animals. And now you're going to join him in that senseless butchering. You must be losing your mind."

She raised her voice as George ascended the wide stairway.

"Hunting and trapping are for poor farmers and kids. Surely, you must realize this is beneath you. And if you would avoid this degrading behavior, perhaps our son would come home and be a part of our family."

A worried frown showed on his colorless face as he entered the bedroom. Resting on the edge of the bed, he caught his breath. "God, I'm tired. Do I really have to attend this political bash tonight?"

He fidgeted as he untied his shoes and changed into formal

37

attire. "For five years now I've wanted to go with my son and learn how he hunts geese and traps in the marsh. And at last I'm going. This social stuff is going to move aside.

"I do agree with Martha on one point. I don't know where these yearnings emanate. Why is Scott drawn to the signs of geese, raccoons, and muskrats? I have never hunted or trapped, and neither have our recent forebears. They have followed lives on cobbled streets, on carpeted floors in offices and courtrooms, eaten fancy foods, and slept every night of their lives under a roof and on a soft bed."

Responding to his wife's call, he slid into his black topcoat and hurried down the carpeted stairs. Offering Martha his arm, he and his wife left the house.

As George drove to the club, his perception of the traffic was vague, for he had closed his mind to Martha's chatter and drifted into the philosophies of hunting.

"Maybe this yen," he thought, "this urge to catch animals and fish, lies dormant in many of us. For sure as I sit here, everyone of us have ancestors who hunted, fished, and trapped. And for thousands of generations. One thing is certain, if they hadn't we wouldn't exist today."

As the couple entered the club, an overwhelming hum of voices, clinking of glasses and muffled violins blanketed their heads. They drifted through the crowd, greeting those they recognized and accepting champagne from gaudily clothed hostesses.

Spotting a tray of hors d'oeuvres, George whispered in Martha's ear. "Better avoid that pate. Goose liver."

"George, you're impossible! Domesticated animals are different from wild ones!"

The balding lawyer frowned. "Oh, are they? Really. Well, we'd better congratulate friend Dorquet before he gets too high to remember."

By twisting through the crowd, the couple located the senator and extended their best wishes. Their meeting was brief, however, because of the great pressure from others seeking favors from the new senator.

Spotting their old friends Fred and Denise Nicolas, George and Martha led them to seats near the front table. The foursome struggled through an almost endless dinner that was choked with accolades and rosy predictions.

Covering a yawn, Fred nudged his wife and rose. "We've got to go. Enjoyed your company, and tell that son of yours to come home once in a while. We'd like to see him, especially Heather."

George also rose. "Well I'll be spending a week with Scott. Going to take a much needed vacation."

Martha's eyes bored into George's. "Some vacation! Going to that hunting camp in the middle of nowhere!"

George tightened his jaw. "Well, it will be a complete change. We'd better leave too, Martha."

Following a laborious Saturday at his office, George battled the increasing fatigue and rose early the following day. He stuffed two small bags and set them by the front door. A flicker of anticipation brightened his anxious face as he kissed his wife.

"Be home next Sunday, Doll, late."

Martha looked beyond his shoulder. "Get some rest, George. And talk Scott into something other than wasting his life in that horrid swamp. Please. He needs to be here with us."

"Well, I'll mention it. Maybe he'll get home for Thanksgiving."

With her voice quavering, Martha squeezed her husband's forearm. "It would mean a lot to me, George."

Seated by a window on the United 727, George found relaxation difficult to induce. Pending cases, aggressive clients, and election aftermath haunted his mind and tightened the core of his body.

As the flight progressed, however, the anxieties eased, and he thought more of his son, the great marsh, and the wildlife his boy described.

"God, what a relief this week will be. No phones, no squabbling, no cheats, no pushing. Believe Scott has the right pursuit after all."

He struggled with his wife's denunciation of killing animals, and tried to fit it in with Scott's biologist view. "He maintains we all must kill living things or die. Life could not go on without it. So how could it be wrong?

"The worst part is that Martha is ashamed of Scott. Being a wildlife biologist, he has no status in Long Island society, and he kills animals, a lowly pursuit in the eyes of the elite socialites.

"Well, I'm proud of my son. His life is open, sincere, and untwisted. A far cry from the millions in the social whirl who lie, cheat, steal, and use others to gain power and wealth."

Disembarking at the Great Basin Airport, George searched for his son's heavy blonde hair and wild sandy beard.

"Dad! Over here!"

George spotted Scott's waving hand and met him with a crazy hug that lifted the towering youth off the floor.

"Is it ever good to see you, Scott. You're looking great. How is it going?"

"Super, Dad. Lots of ducks piling into the refuge. And hundreds of geese. Fat rats by the hundreds, too."

The son stared at his father's countenance, now grayish white and troubled. "Anything wrong, Dad? You alright?"

George stopped and leaned against the terminal wall, trying to smile. "Guess you're too big to pick up anymore, Son. 'Specially in this thin air. But a rest here will do wonders. I'll be ready to go home and whip 'em all."

"By the way, your mother sure would like to see you, or hear your voice. Suppose you could give her a ring?"

Scott looked through the wide windows at the giant jets outside. "Can do. But first, you and I have to visit some noisy geese. And run the rat line, okay?"

Nodding agreement, George gave Scott his bags and the two made their way to the 4X4 pickup to begin the long drive to the refuge.

For Martha, the first days of the week dragged. "Those men just don't care. Here it is Wednesday night and they haven't even sent a card. They are exasperating."

Hearing the musical note of the dining room phone, she jumped from her chair. "Why, it's Scott! How wonderful of you to call! How are you? Are you coming home?"

Scott's voice sounded weak and strange amid the crackling and hissing of the rural line. "I'm calling about Dad."

Martha's mouth remained open in wonderment. "Yes? What about George?"

The static popped louder than before. "Dad's gone. His heart collapsed. He waited too long to get some rest."

Scott fought to stifle a sob. "Really, Mom, it was that insane social life that got Dad. He couldn't take it."

"But you'll be coming home, won't you, Scott? I need you here. Desparately."

Scott's low voice mixed with the hiss of the line. "No, Mom. Sorry. Maybe to visit. My life is here. I don't want the life Dad had."

CHAPTER VII

WHITE BEARD

At the edge of Hardens Marsh, Leo Martin smiled all over as he stuffed another muskrat into his pack. "Nuthin' like foggy weather for ketchin' rats," the eleven year old thought as he peered into the gloom. "Bet I'll get a couple more this morning."

The thin youth skipped along the edge of the cattails, his enthusiasm running high and crowding out weird tales of the endless swamp and the giant hermit who lived there.

Wading through shallow water toward a bait set, Leo felt his head lighten, a slight but ominous warning that he knew so well. "Should've ate somethin' for breakfast," he thought. "I know I should always eat somethin' after my insulin. But I felt half sick. Anyway I've got an orange in my pack and that'll fix me up."

Spotting a purplish form under the water at his next set, Leo retrieved the body trap that held a small rat. The boy labored more than usual in releasing the animal and resetting the trap.

He flinched as a trio of mallards split the fog above him. "What was that?" he asked himself. "Oh, just ducks." He was unable, however, to shake off the anxieties that were creeping into his thoughts. "Heck, Ol' White Beard don't come down this far," he thought. "This ain't his land."

The boy shivered as another flock of ducks whistled above him and the tales of the swamp giant rose in his mind. "Mean, big, ruthless," Leo whispered. "He's stomped many a man into the muck and they were never found. This was his land. No one dared enter. Yeah, he ate fish, rats, and beavers raw, and even though he had only one eye, he could see for miles in the dark.

"Better eat my orange," the boy thought. "Gettin' fuzzier." Reaching into his pack he searched for the fruit. "Gone! Oh, no! Where is my orange? Better head for home. Gotta get some food before I get too weak and dizzy."

Rising, the narrow-faced youth draped his pack over his left shoulder and trudged through the deepening fog. "Boy, these

43

paths all look the same," he thought, blinking and staring. "But I guess this is the right one."

A gust of wind swirled dense clouds over the cattails, rattling the stalks and rippling the water. In the wet air, more ducks cracked the atmosphere as they sought a place to land. Shuffling along a faint trail, Leo's mouth drooped and his slow-moving eyes struggled to find a familiar landmark in the flowing gloom.

"White Beard!" he screamed, staring at a light silhouette near the edge of the cattails. "Go away! Go away!" Trembling, the boy backed from the apparition, gaping in disbelief.

The wind swept away the fog and exposed the object. "Oh, just a dead tree. Sure looked like the giant. Lordy, I gotta get moving!"

The swishing of flying ducks, increasing wind, and waning energy intensified the boy's concerns. He broke into a stumbling trot, fearful now of every patch of fog and raspy cattails. "Gotta get home fast, outa this slough, away from White Beard. Where is that fence, anyway? Should have reached it by now."

With his senses dulled, Leo stared into the fog, searching every opening for the face of White Beard. As he ran, his legs turned into rubber, and he crashed into a brush covered ditch. Shaken, the youth raised his head and looked into the hairy face of the old hermit.

The youth tried to scream, but the great fear stifled his voice. He stared in silent terror as the huge hands of White Beard reached for his throat.

In the kitchen of the Martin home, Leo's father Karl zipped his canvas coat. "Leo's gonna be alright, Marie. He's no dummy. He's run these traps many times."

Mrs. Martin continued to frown. "Yes, but this time, it's different. Downright serious. He's never been this late. And from what I can see, he's had no breakfast. You know what can happen if he goes without eating."

Karl eased out the kitchen door. "No need to worry, Marie. The boy always carries a little food in his pack. Well, I'm off. I'll either find him or he'll get home on his own."

Reaching the edge of the slough, Karl slowed his pace and searched for signs of his son. "Don't know where he went, but he had to travel this edge. He knew he wasn't to wade out very far."

Zigzagging along the path, Karl noticed some muddy tracks in the water and stopped to examine them. "They gotta be Leo's!" he thought, and reassured, he increased his pace along the winding path.

Stopping again, his face turned vacant. "An orange! Good lord, he must've dropped it," Karl thought. "But maybe he had another one. I don't see any peels, though."

With rising concern, Karl rushed along the trail, his eyes darting back and forth, looking for indications of Leo. He searched several forks that split from the main trail but discovered nothing. As the fog lifted, Karl knelt to rest and he studied the vast, endless marsh. "Sure no sign here," he thought. "Could he have gone home a different way? Not likely. I'd better go back and get some help, really comb this slough."

Swinging through the back gate, Karl banged up the porch and into the kitchen. His face was grave.

"Did Leo show up yet?"

Marie stopped kneading the soft, cream-colored dough, and leaned on the heavy board. Her face, too, was solemn.

"Yes, he got home, and he's okay, gone to school." The mother's gaze fell onto the dough. "But you must realize he had a really close call. Almost passed out on his feet and got lost. Just lucky that old trapper found him and brought him home."

Karl slumped into the heavy oak chair.

"Well, that's a relief. Who found him, old Sam Dobbins?"

Marie let a little smile show on her face. "Yes, the one the kids call White Beard."

CHAPTER VIII

IN THE DARK

Old Snooks Crow had always figgered himself to be a mountain man. He'd spent many a night on the upper Rio Grande with only a horse blanket for cover, eatin' muskrat and wadin' icy creeks wet. Plus, he ran his traps in the dark, claimin' he could see better'n a cat.

Snooks started flounderin' without a light early. When he was twelve years old and runnin' his traps with no light, he bent over to check a set. Zap! He got skunked in the face.

Well, he banged himself so bad from trippin' through the brush tryin' to get to water, he swore he'd learn to do most anythin' in the dark.

So Snooks kept a runnin' his trap line with a little pen light or no light at all. He faunched through the chico chasin' grappled coyotes, felt his way through rocks listen'n for hooked cats, and splashed along the Rio Grande checkin' beaver and rat sets.

Snooks learned to dress, go to the bathroom, and raid the 'frigerator with no light. In doin' early morning chores, he'd work with as little light as he could. Later, he figgered how to find hidden whiskey bottles in the closet by fumble and feel.

But slick as he was, Snooks carried a few scars from his nightly forays. His toenails were split, shins scarred, face dented. His wife, too, suffered bad, nearly losin' her mind from the bangin' and squallin' in the night.

Snooks' lightless sojourns made their marks on the house, too, leavin' busted lamps, bunged chairs, and slops all over, 'specially on the bathroom floor.

Now every fall, Snooks laid out a bunch of iron for them crazy wild dogs. Even in his late years, he kept a settin' in the chico along the banks of the Rio Grande.

In makin' coyote sets, he'd use grapples wherever there was brush close by. 'Cause, you see, he got a bang outa findin' the critters in the dark without a light. He'd track 'em by sound, listen'n for a clink of chain or a crackle of brush.

The faunchin' and thrashin' of a hooked dog in the dark sure raised the hair on his neck, 'specially if the coyote laid low until Snooks got real close and then broke loose with his lungin'. Now and then Snooks wouldn't find a dog 'til after sun-up, makin' him late for mornin' chores. His missus wasn't understandin' on such days, 'cause she'd get stuck with the work. Although she'd squall louder than a mashed cat, her shriekin' had little effect on Snooks.

One Saturday in early November, Snooks was plannin' to haul some heifers to the sale barn, bein' due there by mid-mornin'. Trouble was, though, that mid mornin' had already passed and he hadn't come home from his trapline.

Havin' finished the mornin' chores, the missus was settin' in the kitchen frettin' and stewin'. "Now what's he up to this mornin'," she thought. "Out there trapsin' after them goofy coyotes instead of gettin' the cows to town."

Watchin' out the kitchen window, she kept a grumblin' while she sipped some scaldin' coffee. "If he don't come soon, I'll have to haul them heifers myself," she thought. "Maybe I ought to get 'em loaded."

Hearing the rattle of an old pickup, she jumped up and grabbed her coat. "There he is now! About time."

Her teeth was a grindin' as she approached the pickup, and she appeared not to notice the giant badger that Snooks was liftin' from the bed of the truck.

"Just where have you been? And when are you gonna get them heifers to town? It's already past ten now!"

Noticing Snooks' colorless face, she held her scoldin' and spoke in a quiet voice. "So that's what you been chasin'. A big 'un. And I suppose he run for miles and miles."

Snooks hands trembled as he hung the huge digger to a beam in the implement shed. "Yeah. He went a ways. Never made a sound. Quiet as the night. Real trouble was the pickup. I got hung up on some cussed rocks."

"You alright, Snooks? Didya do too much walkin' this mornin'?"

Snooks looked away as he rubbed his wrinkled chin. "Nope. The walkin' didn't bother."

"Well, what, then? Couldn't you find 'im 'fore daylight?"

Snooks propped a stiff leg on the pickup bumper, squeezing his calf with huge hands. "Nope. Found 'im 'fore daylight alright. And without a light."

Displayin' a weak grin, the agin' trapper lifted his left pant leg and squinted at the raw gash on his ankle. "But not until he found me!"

CHAPTER IX

BEARDS AND TRAPS

In the dense fog of early morning, Jimmy Ray Hawkins and his younger brother Sammy sloshed along the edge of Muddy Creek, searching for the last of their muskrat sets. He blew drips of water from his nose as he bent and peered under the bank. "This'ns gone, too, Sammy! No stake, no nothin'! Somebody's cleaned us out good!"

The freckle-faced 13-year-old again ran his hand around the entrance to the muskrat den. "That makes twenty traps that's gone. And some had rats in 'em!"

Standing among the purple willow shoots on the high bank, his younger brother, Sammy, frowned. "Bet it's one of them bigtime trappers from town. One that drives all over."

Jimmy Ray stomped up the muddy bank, his boot straps flopping against the brush. "Well, we gotta find this dirty crook. And we'll fix 'im, one way or another."

He scanned the creek bottom and edges of the bank. "Sure don't see any tracks here. But we'd better look some more upstream aways."

The pair continued along the winding stream until they encountered a sagging, rusty fence. Jimmy Ray turned to Sammy. "I think this here place belongs to old Ezra Nolte from town. We ain't got permission to trap here, but maybe it couldn't hurt if we just looked around to see if anyone's settin' here."

As Jimmy Ray raised one leg over the fence, Sammy thumped his back. "Over there! By the big sycamore!"

Flinching, Jimmy Ray hooked a boot on the wire and tumbled onto the ground. "If this is one of yer jokes, Sammy, I'll bust you good!"

"No kiddin'! I seen 'im. Carryin' a sack."

The older boy rose, and peered through the thick fog and dripping hardwoods. "Oh, yeah! There he is, comin' this way! Let's hide and see what he's up to."

51

With pounding hearts, the boys ducked behind a gum tree and lay on the soggy ground. Their bodies tensed as they watched the stranger glide toward them without a sound.

Jimmy Ray lowered his head and whispered, "He must be a trapping, bendin' down like he does. But ain't he ugly with all that black hair and beard!"

Jimmy lifted his head and peeked over the tops of the willows. "Don't see 'im, Sammy. He's gone! But how did he get away so quick?"

Both boys stood and scanned the foggy landscape, wondering how the stranger had disappeared.

Jimmy slung his trap sack over his shoulder. "Know what, Sammy? Maybe we ought to see if'n he's got any traps set. To see if they's ours."

Sammy's mouth was tight. "Yeah, but he might be hidin' somewheres up there. Then what?"

"Well, we'll wait a little, then look. He'll be gone by then."

After a short time, Jimmy Ray stepped into the creek and searched several holes and runs. "Here's a couple of traps, Sammy. But they ain't ours. They're killer traps." Repositioning the traps, Jimmy Ray stepped from the stream.

"Well, we'd better take up what traps we have left and go home. Can't leave 'em here. We'll just lose the rest."

Arriving at the farm home, the brothers shuffled into the weathered tool shed where Dan Hawkins was bent over a dismantled engine. The boys greeted their dad and dumped the sacks on the bench. In rapid breaths, they told of the missing traps and the bearded suspect.

Dan left the engine and put his hands on his sons' shoulders. "It's gonna be tough, boys, findin' your traps, even though we have our brands on 'em. And just see'n that trapper close by don't mean he took 'em."

Returning to the ailing motor, the father fitted a long-handled socket onto a stubborn manifold bolt. "If I'm not mistaken, there's a second-hand junk dealer south of town who wears a heavy black beard. Believe he buys some furs and he might sell traps. Maybe we better pay him a visit." He looked at Jimmy Ray over the tops of his glasses.

"Where's your friend, Orly? Didn't he come today?"

"Naw. The other week he fell in, and got mad 'cause we laughed at 'im. Besides, he's gittin' lazy since he quit school. Don't seem to like trappin' anymore."

The following Saturday, Dan Hawkins and his sons drove to the home of the second-hand dealer. Parking amongst the heaps of junk, the trio wound their way to the garage. They knocked and entered the open door.

The sweet musk of rats mixed with the heavier odor of skunk hung in the damp air of the shed. In the rear of the building, a tall, bearded man frowned as he struggled to pull a thick hide from a boar coon. Hearing the visitors approach, he straightened and rubbed his hip. "What can I do for you folks?"

"Howdy. Was wondering if you had any used leg-hold traps for rats?"

The dealer eyed the boys and then the father. "Nope. None that size. All I got is 2's and 3's. You might find some at Hartley's in town. He handles traps."

Dan searched the boys' faces, then the dealer's. "You do any trappin'? Or you just buy furs?"

"Don't trap much anymore. Can't get around too good, on account of this hip."

"Well, thanks. C'mon boys, we gotta go."

As the pickup eased out the drive, the boys spoke with dejected voices. "That ain't him, Dad. He just don't look like the man we seen."

Dan shifted into high gear. "I agree. Don't believe he walks much. Well, we'll just have to keep lookin'. Something will show up."

During the following week, Jimmy Ray and Sammy scouted neighboring farms looking for clues as to who might have taken their traps. Travelling separately, they searched in the early hours before school.

On Friday morning, Jimmy Ray stood by the round oak kitchen table fidgeting with his books. "Now where is that Sammy? If he don't come quick, we'll miss the bus. I'd better go." Opening the back door, Jimmy was struck by a racing breathless Sammy.

"I seen 'im! I seen 'im! A settin' in the ditch!"

Rising from the knockdown, Jimmy Ray regained his footing. "Wait a minute. Just calm down. Who'd you see? And where at?"

Sammy gaped at Jimmy Ray, his breaths rapid, his face wild. "Black beard! In the ditch at Holman's slough. I know it was him. Plain as day!"

Jimmy Ray glanced at the kitchen clock and gulped. "C'mon. We'd better get to the bus. After seeing McCracken's Saturday, we'll go to Holman's and see if he knows this guy."

Finishing their Saturday morning's work, the two boys returned to the kitchen of the brick farmhouse to meet their friend Orly Wilts.

"Howdy, Orly. Like I told you on the phone, we're gonna ask Mr. McCracken if'n we can set in his slough. There's rats there. And it'll be safe from thieves, hid away from everything. We had to pull out of Muddy Creek, gittin' ripped off so bad."

As the trio hiked along the back road to the McCracken property, the brothers told Orly more details of the missing traps and the stranger with the black beard.

Sammy hustled to hold his own with the fast stepping of the older boys.

"Yeah, and you know, Orly, that guy disappeared into the fog like magic. And yesterday, he was gone just as fast into clear air!"

Orly turned to Jimmy Ray. "He sure sounds slick. But how do you s'pose he found your rat sets?"

Jimmy shrugged his shoulders. "Well, I dunno for sure. But with all that rat sign and him bein' a trapper, he's bound to know where to set. And there's wires and stakes that show. Them's dead giveaways."

As the youths arrived at the McCracken farm, they met Mrs. McCracken at the side door. "We was wonderin' if we could get permission to trap rats on your slough, Mrs. McCracken?"

The old woman tried to clear her throat. "You boys Hawkins?"

"Yep. And this is Orly Wilts. From Waterboro."

"Well, Mr. McCracken ain't home just now. But he's already let someone trap there. On shares. He come in real early and left in a few days. Strange lookin' man. Tall with a big black beard. Never did get 'is name."

Jimmy Ray stared at the woman's thin, wrinkled face. "Black beard, huh? Yeah. Well, thanks anyway, Mrs. McCracken. We'll be goin'."

Disappointed from such news, the boys trudged out the drive, scuffing gravel and looking at the ground. Jimmy kicked a small rock into the ditch. "That crook must trap everywhere. He's hoggin' all the places, as well as traps. Well, guess there's no use in going to Holman's. He's probably been there, too."

At dinner that evening, Dan Hawkins' face was serious as his sons related their encounter with Mrs. McCracken.

"Seems as though this bearded fellow is coverin' a lot of country. But sooner or later, we'll find out who he is. In the meantime, we'll just keep lookin'."

Bitter cold air settled on the Hawkins' farm that night, covering the trees and buildings with heavy frost. The cold held its grip well after sunrise, and nipped the boys' ears and fingers as they ran through their Sunday chores.

Finishing their work, they stuffed their numbed hands in their pockets and hurried toward the house. In front of the rear gate, they observed a silver 4X4 Ford pickup in the drive. Their pulses pounded as a black-bearded giant crawled from the cab. "Does Dan Hawkins live here?"

The boys stared at the stranger, unable to reply. They melted toward the gate as their father opened the kitchen door. "Howdy. I'm Dan Hawkins. What can I do for you?"

The giant offered his hand. "I'm Jeff Driscoll, new here in Waterboro. I trap some, but my main business is buying furs."

54

"Well, we don't sell to locals. We ship to auctions."

"That's not the reason I'm here. I came about some traps. Stoploss, branded on the bottom left. Are you missin' some?" Dan answered in a whisper. "Well, yeah. About twenty were stolen couple of weeks ago. How'd you know?" The buyer's white teeth shone through the jumble of black hair. "Well, a week or so ago, some fellow in town was sellin' a few rats and wanted to know if I bought traps. Now, I don't mess with second-hand traps, but I looked at 'em out of curiosity. I noticed they was branded and when I asked if this was his mark, he got real nervous, and didn't answer. So I was gettin' suspicious and checked the brand with the State Trappers Association. They said the brand was yours."

Dan and the boys searched each others' faces. "Yeah, that's my brand alright," said Dan. "But who is this fellow?"

"Got his name right here. Wilts. Orly Wilts."

CHAPTER X

THE NEWCOMER

On a clear, bright Sunday in October, the sun warmed the parishioners and interior of the Community Church in Springfield. The young Arnette boys, Sid and Dale, stood by their mother, Lora, as the congregation sang the opening hymn. Dressed in spotless Sunday attire and exuding a faint odor of skunk, the black haired twins held a hymnal and stared at Tony Slezak, a young newcomer in the next pew.

With subtle movements, Sid withdrew a small bottle from his pocket and hid it in the half-closed songbook. Then he shook a black tarantula from the bottle onto the page and covered it with his hand. With his lower lip wet and quivering, he lifted his hand and flicked the hairy spider toward the slick dressed boy in front.

Sid's eyes popped as the spider veered to the right. "Oh, no!" he thought. "It landed on Mrs. Almstead! Lordy, what will I do now?"

Peppy from the heat and new freedom, the tarantula zipped across the woman's heavy arm, over her white blouse, and into the valley of her giant bosom.

Spotting the fleeting arthropod, the stout woman's eyes bulged as panic swept through her immense body. Her strong soprano voice rose to a high pitched yodel that drowned out the other singers. With wild, frenzied hands, she threw the hymnal into the air and dug at her blouse, popping the buttons and exposing the crouching spider. In a mighty sweep of her right hand, she knocked the tarantula to the floor where it disappeared.

Holding her blouse closed, the trembling woman stomped from the pew and left the golden, sunfilled church.

Except for wide eyes and pounding hearts, the Arnette boys succeeded in appearing calm. Inside, the pre-teenagers were filled with cold, clammy terror, stunned at the unexpected turn

57

of events.

"Keep lookin' straight ahead," Sid thought. "Don't look at Mom. She'll know from our faces. Why is the pastor staring at us? How could he know? This is gettin' sweaty."

As the ruckus subsided, Lora Arnette, the Slezaks, and other members of the congregation wrinkled their brows, wondering what caused the panicky exit of Mrs. Almstead.

Suspecting that the twins might know something of the disturbance, Lora Arnette hurried home after church and dug out the truth. In an explosion of anger, she pulled hair and whacked bottoms. "What is the matter with you two? That poor woman almost died of fright! And the boy did nothing to you. Just because he is new is no excuse. You treat him right, d'ya hear? And you go nowhere for two weeks!"

She flopped into a kitchen chair to catch her breath and pushed graying hair from her face. "Now you get over to Mrs. Almstead and apologize. You hurt her bad. And you will do some work for her, whatever she says."

With their hair dishevelled and bottoms hurting, the thin-faced twins eased out the back door and made their way to Martha Almstead's to make amends. For their prank, they would have to clean her yard this fall and next spring.

Pouring herself a cup of coffee, Lora went into the living room and collapsed on the flowered sofa. She ran her fingers through her coarse hair as she stared at the gray and golden fields through the picture window.

"How will I ever face that poor woman?" she thought. "And what will I ever do with those wild kids? They're getting worse. Lord, they just got through with staying after school a week for hiding a fat girl's lunch. And that was on top of stuffing rotten eggs on the manifold of the school janitor's pickup."

Her eyes fell onto the brown carpeted floor. "I was hoping chores and odd jobs would keep them busy," she reasoned. "And it does, some. But they still pull these crazy stunts, scaring people with snakes and lizards, squabbling over nothing, screaming and mauling each other with sticks, tools, and rat carcasses. Yes, I can still feel that slimy rat carcass hitting me in the face when I tried to stop one of their melees.

"And that fracas they had getting skunk essence from a carcass. One of them cutting and the other squeezing around the back end, trying to drip some into a jar. What a terrible row that caused! Those two were covered with stink and guts, all over their faces, hair, and clothes. Lord, they still smell!"

She sighed after draining her cup. "It sure would help if their dad was home more, instead of on the road most of the time. Really, though, the kids do work hard and are well mannered most of the time. If they just weren't so ornery. Well, I have to keep bearing down on them or they'll never straighten up."

When their confinement ended, the energetic twins raced to the river to place their traps, and, in spite of the late start, they caught good numbers of muskrats and a few raccoons. Too, they hooked a young coyote after battling frozen ground for a week.

At dawn on Veterans Day, Lora stood over her cast iron grill baking hot cakes for Sid and Dale. As the boys sat at the table, she set a plate of steaming cakes in front of them. "I met Tony Slezak's mother yesterday. She told me that her boy would like to learn about trapping. And I was thinking you two could take him along and show him how. He doesn't know much about it, having come from Aurora."

Dales's brown eyes shot to Sid as he set the sticky syrup bottle next to his plate. "If we show him our traps, he'll just come back and steal 'em."

"I don't think so, Dale. You don't have to show him your sets. Just show him how to set his."

Sid refused to yield to his mother's demanding face. "Do we have to, Mom?"

After a long silence, Sid could see no change. "Yeah, okay, Mom. We'll show 'im. But he don't get to see any of our sets." He slid more cakes on his plate and reached for the syrup. "Guess we'd better do it Saturday. Get it over with. I'll tell 'im at school."

On the weekend, Tony rendezvoused with the slight built twins at the Arnette home. In the damp, gray cold of mid-morning, the trio rode on their bikes to a dump near the winding, slow moving river where the two youths explained how to make a bank hole set.

Sid pointed to the trap. "You gotta put it inside the hole so's it won't freeze. And wiggle it into the dirt so's it won't flop around. Then cover it with fine grass and leaves. Now for the bait. This fish oil is tops. Just pour some in the back of the hole. Here, you do it."

The stocky, brown haired youth took the jar, knelt, and dribbled some oil into the back of the hole. "Whew! Sure stinks! Do coons really like this stuff?"

"Yeah, they love it. Skunks, too."

Taking the jar from Tony, Sid tipped the bottle and spilled some on the newcomer's brand new jeans.

"Whoops, slopped a little there. Sorry. We'd better try a couple of coyote sets. Closer to the dump."

Tony gulped as he stared at the blotches of oil on his trousers. "Boy," he thought, "how am I gonna get that stuff off my pants?"

Closer to the dump, the twins showed Tony how to make dirt sets for coyotes using his large, rusted longspring traps. After adding some of their homemade lure, the Arnettes returned to the river and helped Tony place some of his large traps for muskrats. In setting a trap in the entrance of a rat's den, Tony slipped on the muddy slope and fell into the icy water. Scrambling up the bank, he gasped for air. "Wooee! It's like ice! It's so cold it hurts!"

Noticing Tony's violent shivering, Sid slipped out of his coat. "Here, Tony, put this on."

Hesitating, Tony looked at Sid, then at the dry coat. "Well, okay, that'd sure feel good."

As the boys readied to leave, Sid put his hand on Tony's shoulder. "Now, there's somethin' you gotta remember about skunks. In case you catch one. You gotta break their necks so's they won't squirt all that stink when they die. So you hit 'em hard right behind the head. To break their neck. Okay?"

Tony wrinkled his face and sniffed his runny nose. "Yeah, I guess so. Is that the way you kill 'em?"

"Well, if we catch one, we shoot 'em with a twenty-two and let 'em lay a day or two to air out."

Shivering, Tony put his hands into the jacket pockets. "Well, I ain't got a twenty-two, so I guess I'll have to use a stick."

Having finished, the boys mounted their bikes and struck for home, Tony trembling all the way and splitting from the twins at the edge of town. At their small, white stucco house, the boys parked their well worn bikes and tromped into the kitchen looking for a noon meal.

Seeing the pair enter, Lora lifted some chicken noodle soup into wide tan colored bowls. "Well, how'd things go today?"

Dale was first at the sink to wash. "Good, Mom. We caught three rats."

Lora set the steaming bowls on the table. "I mean, how did you and Tony get along?"

Sid glanced at Dale, then at his mother. "Yeah, okay. Tony's a good sport. But he don't know much about settin'. And all he's got is big traps. But we showed him how to set for rats, coon, and coyote."

Lora's eyes bored into his. "You didn't pull any nasties, did you?"

Sid lowered his head. "Oh, no. Just showed 'im how to set." He looked at Dale, his head still down. "Course he fell in settin' for rats. Accidentally. He got a little wet but he didn't mind. Thought it was fun."

"Oh, yes, I'll bet he did. What else?"

Blowing on his soup, Dale hid a grin as he squeaked an answer. "Well, he spilled a little bait on his new Levis. That's all."

Lora pulled a chair from the table and sat at her place. "Now, you two listen. You did right by showing Tony how to set. And I'm pleased. But the ornery stuff was unnecessary. And no more, d'ya here?"

Sid sucked some hanging noodles from his spoon and frowned. "Heck, Mom, if Tony's gonna be a trapper, he's gotta get used to bein' wet now and then. And smellin' a little."

"Well, no more, that's it."

After school the following Friday, Sid and Dale hurried home and banged up the steps of the back porch. Sid shuddered as he noticed his mother waiting at the door. "Oh, oh, somethin's up, Dale. Mom looks mad," he whispered.

Lora's arms were folded over her bosom. "Yes, I'm mad. You boys been treating that Tony like trash. He came home from his trap line this morning reeking worse than a hundred mangled skunks. Couldn't go to school, and half his hide gone from his mother trying to scrub off the stink.

"And his mother is mad, too. She gave me the works for a half hour about you boys telling Tony how to kill a skunk." The tall, large-boned woman dropped her hands to her hips. "Surely you told him how to take a skunk out of the trap without getting stunk up. Or did you?"

Dale stopped swinging his books. "Yeah, we did, Mom. We told him to be sure to break the skunk's neck with a stick. So's he wouldn't squirt. Honest."

"Yes, but why a stick? Why not a twenty-two like you boys use?"

Sid took the lead. "But, Mom, he doesn't have a twenty-two. So how else could he kill 'im, 'cept with a stick?"

Her voice softened. "Well, you could have offered to kill it with your rifle. Seems like telling him to club a skunk is the worst thing you could have done."

She turned to enter the house. "Remember that Tony's an adopted boy. Just like you two. So go over and help him with skinning the smelly thing. And if you pull any more crazy tricks, you'll stay home for a year!"

The tall, graying woman quieted as she prepared supper. "Lord, what next?" she thought. "Just when I thought they were improving. I'm just about at my wit's end. Well, their father will be home this weekend and maybe he will have some influence."

A week later, the twins sat with Tony in the school lunchroom. "So you're not having much luck, Tony?" Sid asked. "Well, maybe you need to freshen up your sets."

Tony popped a cookie into his mouth and spoke with a low voice. "Yeah, I sure need somethin'. If I could just catch a coyote, then I'd be a real trapper."

"Well, tell you what," Dale said, closing his blue lunch bucket. "We can meet you at the dump sometime. To help you with your sets. With some extra stinky lure."

A faint half grin brightened Tony's face. "Would you? Boy, that'd be great!"

On the day after Thanksgiving, Lora and her husband lingered in the kitchen after a late breakfast. "Well, this wet snow should keep the kids busy, shovelling walks and driveways. And your being home, Clayton, will help keep them on their good behavior. It really will. Guess I'd better thaw some burgers for the boys' lunch."

As Lora searched the freezer for a package of ground beef, Clayton responded to the front door bell. "Yes, Lora's home. Please come in, Mrs. Slezak."

Wiping her hands on her scarlet apron, Lora remained at the freezer and stared at the frosty interior. "Oh, dear," she thought. "Why is she here? Have the boys pulled another trick on Tony? They've been so good lately. Well, they will pay dearly if they have caused trouble."

Tightening her lips, she drifted toward the front door. "Why, hello, Mrs. Slezak. How are you? And Tony?"

The short, wiry haired woman stared at Lora, her face expressionless. "I came to talk about your twins."

"Oh, no, not again," she thought. "Yes, what about them? Did they cause trouble?"

Mrs. Slezak's face remained blank. "No, Mrs. Arnette. Last weekend, they helped Tony make a set for coyote. Around a dead horse, I think. And, you know, this morning he caught a coyote. I want you to know that he is one pleased boy."

A gentle smile warmed her face. "It sure was good of your boys to show Tony such a good place to set. He'll not forget it, I can assure you."

"What a relief," Lora thought, as she scanned her mind for words to reply. "Well, I'm thankful that the boys are getting along. Perhaps they found a common bond after all."

CHAPTER XI

BUSINESS IS BUSINESS

In the winter of '79, a fast talkin' fur buyer made hisself known in the San Luis Valley. Comin' from the hills east of the divide, this slick dealin' peddler learned how to trade early in life, and, although he was new to fur buyin', he'd picked up the tricks fast. In lookin' at furs, he could find pin holes, sewed holes, rips, tears, rubs, and spoilt spots no matter how good they was hid. And, when he was offerin' his insultin' low prices, he would come on with his aggravatin' sayin', "Business is business."

Goin' by the name of Jimmy Malenka, he was gettin' to be known as Squeaky 'cause he was so tight and cheap.

On his third trip through Antonito, the short legged buyer stopped at the cafe on the north edge of town. At the end of the lunch counter, he got to dealin' with a smooth lookin' feller by the name of Vasquez for a real big white fur.

"Ain't never seen a white coyote before," Jimmy was sayin', while he run his stubby fingers through the fur tryin' to feel the crackly skin. "Nor one this big."

Puttin' on his bad market act, Squeaky looked real close at the nose and ears of the hide. "But there just ain't no demand for white coyotes. Pales, yeah. They're good. But this'n wouldn't bring ten dollars."

Squeaky bent his baldin' head down and puckered up like he was gonna bawl. "But I'll tell you what, Vasquez, I'll stick my neck out and give you twenty dollars. That's a heck of a good price."

Well, this here Vasquez wasn't gonna let his fur go cheap, so he picked it up and walked away. "A hundred dollars or nothin'."

Gettin' a wee bit desperate, Squeaky livened up his show, stompin', fussin', fakin' tears, and walkin' off. But Vasquez hung tough, 'cause he was thinkin' that Squeaky wanted this white fur worse'n anythin'.

The squablin' and arguin' went on 'til Squeaky lost his patience and gave in. "Okay, okay, a hundred dollars. But I'm gonna lose my butt on this deal. It's plain robbery."

Well, Vasquez was pleased and then some, but he never cracked a smile, just stuffed the check in his pocket and walked off.

Now Squeaky's real reason for goin' the limit on the white fur was that an oil man from Odessa was offerin' big money fer off color coyotes. So Squeaky figgered on makin' a thousand dollars, maybe more, on the white pelt, and went home with a funny grin on his oily face.

A month later, on his next round of fur buyin', Squeaky buzzed into Antonito like he was in a real big hurry. Parkin' at the cafe where trappers came to sell their furs, he busted through the steamed-up door, lookin' like he had bad indigestion. He glared at the cook behind the counter.

"Where's this Vasquez at? Charlie Vasquez?"

The cook wasn't in no hurry to answer, bein' upset at Squeaky's bad manners.

"I said, where's that Charlie Vasquez live?"

The cook looked out the window and rolled a toothpick around his lips with his tongue. "What you want him for?"

"Business. I gotta see him on business."

The pudgy cook drug it out some more. "What business?"

Squeaky's blood pressure was creepin' up 'cause his face was gettin' dark. "Well, if you wanna know, it's that white coyote he sold me. 'Twarn't no coyote. 'Twas a domestic dog. And I lost a hundred dollars on it. Plus my reputation. Now where's he at?"

The black haired cook leaned on the counter and squinted at the buyer. "How'd you know it wasn't a coyote?"

Squeaky shoved his greasy felt hat around his head and threw hisself into one of them desparation tantrums. " 'Cause some danged expert in Texas examined it and claimed it was a domestic dog. That's why! Killed a helluva good deal! Make you mad enough to eat nails!"

A little grin crept onto the cook's face as he pointed his toothpick as Squeaky. "Well, if it wasn't a coyote, how come you bought it?"

"Hell, that Vasquez sold it for a coyote. And I got took! Ain't never been skinned so bad in all my whole life! He owes me, d'ya hear? Now, where's he at?"

Chucklin', the cook straightened up. "As I remember, Vasquez didn't say it was a coyote. You did. So he ain't to blame."

The cook's saggin' face turned serious. "Just remember, Squeaky, when you deal with Vasquez, business is business. They don't call him Chisler for nothin'."

CHAPTER XII

THE GREAT MINK OF TOMICHI

As dusk fell on upper Tomichi Creek, a large mink bobbed along the snow covered bank, his rapid breaths turning white in the bitter cold air. He moved with ease through the roots of overhanging banks, watching for a careless mouse and sign of muskrats. Occasionally, he dove into a hole in the ice and swam down the stream under the frozen mantle.

Nearing a high bank of an abandoned beaver dam, the great mink slowed and sniffed the air. He stopped and raised his head to get a better whiff of the strange, tempting odor. Then, with slow, quivering steps, he eased toward the hollow log.

His body flinched with alarm as he scented a fearful odor. Steel and man! Backing from the log, he turned toward the creek and travelled down the drainage with giant strides.

His rapid pace carried him a mile below the scented log, and to a series of small dams. Feeling at ease again, he slowed his gait and searched for an entry into the ice. Spotting an opening, he flicked into the hole and swam with the slow current, looking into the darkness for a trout within striking distance. Near an open runway over the dam, the agile mink cornered a small brook trout in a jumble of sticks and mud. With the fish in his mouth, he popped into the opening of the runway and squatted there to eat and survey his territory.

Finishing his evening meal, the giant mink loped down the stream, leaving large crooked prints in the shallow snow. Approaching a small, open spring, close to some large rocks, he noticed a new odor, sweet and heavy with the scent of muskrat and without the odor of man. Feeling secure in open water the mink moved toward the lure, sniffing, looking, wondering. Pausing, he raised and lowered his head to get a better view and a keener scent. Steel! His sharp eyes spotted an uncovered trap beneath the water. Reversing himself in a frenzied whirl, the large mink bounded for the open ice at top speed. Oh, yes, he knew the danger of rusted iron. Years ago, he bored into a similar spring laden with spicy lure and blundered into a half covered trap. That mistake nearly cost him his life and left his right rear foot askew. No, he would never forget the sight nor the scent of iron!

In wild panic, the mink raced across the snow covered ice, looking for a familiar runway he had used many times before and where he could travel unseen under the ice. Seeing the hole, he dove into the narrow opening at high speed, never noticing the nearby tracks of man nor the partially hidden trap under the water.

The mink exploded into the air as the iron slammed against his crippled rear foot and he crashed against the ice. His heart raced as he lurched against the unyielding trap and chain, back and forth, into the runway, and along the edge of the ice. Through the night, his body remained filled with fear, and as his energy waned, he lost much of his physical power.

Just before dawn, the distant hoot of a great horned owl generated new fear into the tiring body of the great mink. He knew the danger of this powerful avian hunter that struck in the dark, for several times he had escaped the owl by diving into the water ahead of the plummeting talons.

But now he was exposed on top of the ice, with little water in which to escape and little freedom to dodge the piercing claws. He listened and watched with apprehension as he circled to free himself, tiring more with each turn.

As the call of the owl ceased, a thin sliver of moon rose in the east and the mink no longer worried about the winged foe. His fears now came from approaching daylight, for he would be exposed to more enemies, such as man, dogs, and hawks.

He renewed his thrashing against the trap, never realizing that the bones of the crippled toes were now severed and only a shred of tough skin held him. Tiring again, he slowed his lunging and awaited a flow of new strength.

As the light of dawn illuminated the white landscape, the great mink felt a new surge of fear. Men! Two of them! Heading toward him!

He lunged again and again in all directions, trying to shake the tenacious iron and elude the oncoming men. He thrashed and jumped until his muscles failed to respond. Exhausted he sat on his haunches and eyed his captors at close range.

The giant mink bared his teeth and hissed at the two pack-laden men, awaiting whatever fate had in store. He hissed again as the larger man knelt before him. Face to face, the mink and the man searched each others' eyes.

Rising, the large man studied the thread of skin that barely held the mink, and rested his hand on the small one's shoulder. The two stared at the mink, wondering at what they saw.

"Well, Son, this is one huge mink. Biggest I've ever seen. But we don't need him. He's a cotton mink and his fur isn't worth much. We'll let him go and maybe he will father some good dark mink next year."
The exhausted animal flew into one last fit of desperate lunging. As the heavy body lurched, the last shred of skin gave way, and the mink tumbled over the dam. There he recovered and with irregular strides, he loped across the ice, his splotchy grey and white fur looking strange on the body of such a great mink.

CHAPTER XIII

THE GHOST OF TRAPPER JOHN

As a boy, Frankie Salermo learned how to survive on the streets of Pueblo. Before he was five, the agile youth could stack cards and deal from the bottom. He figured how to jump high fences, run through dark alleys, and lie with an innocent face. After several beatings, the slim youth never picked fights alone. Instead, he travelled with friends who fought dirty and could outrun the cops and fast-stepping gangs.

Although Frankie's mind was sharp, he quit school when he was 15. Being unemployed and ducking in and out of trouble, he tortured his guardian Aunt Tet until she almost lost her mind.

Hoping an out of town trip might help, the aging aunt persuaded Frankie to visit his cousins in southwest Colorado. Knowing that the Stutkas kept their children, Isaac and Marie, busy on the ranch, Aunt Tet reasoned that they could do the same for her nephew. "Maybe Frankie would take to ridin' horses and chasin' cows instead of devilin' cops," she thought.

Because they hadn't seen each other for some time, the sunburned Stutkas were anxious to show their city cousin all about life on the ranch. On the first day, they put Frankie to work catching and wrestling calves that were to be branded. Being soft, Frankie's body hurt like a boil at the end of the day, and he wondered why he had come to the ranch.

At the end of the second day, hazel-eyed Marie put the aching cousin on her bay horse. "This'll help loosen up them sore muscles. Now sit back and turn him like I showed you."

Frankie handled the horse like a pro in the corral, but outside, his bronc wasn't as friendly and a whole lot faster. Unable to stay on, Frankie cursed the balky horse and the hard landings in the dirt. "How'm I gonna stay on this jumpin' jack?"

During the next two weeks, after working fences and corrals during the day, Frankie rode the lively bay in the evenings. With Marie's help, he figured how to hang on and began to get a kick out of riding.

After a couple of overnight rides together, Isaac and Marie thought that Frankie ought to learn to work alone and stay by himself overnight. "Hell, nothin to it," Frankie said. "I can roost anywhere by myself."

On the next long ride, the Stutkas furnished Frankie with a map, sleeping gear, and some grub. At sundown, they dropped their cousin at an old cabin near the mouth of Cañon Diablo. After agreeing to meet there in the morning, Isaac and Marie rode to another camp farther west.

Earlier, at the ranch house, the slow moving father, Tony, had told his favorite tale about Cañon Diablo. His wrinkled face had showed no emotion as he talked. "Yep, Frankie, an old trapper named John lived in these parts years ago. Lived, that is, until a mad bear crashed in the door and killed 'im. Gobbled him up, all 'cept his boots. Nothin' left but boots and blood. Lots a' blood."

The old man had narrowed his eye as he continued. "Old timers say that the bear got his toes pinched in one of Old John's Newhouse traps and went berserk. The bear, bein' so big, threw the trap in a violent fit of thumpin' and thrashin', churnin' the snow into the tops of the fir trees, bustin' off saplin's, and bellerin' until the ground shook.

"The rampagin' bear stomped through the forest with his jaws open and growlin' with every breath. As he crossed Old John's trail, he sniffed the track and followed it to the cabin. There he broke through the door and finished off the old man."

Wondering at Frankie's expressionless face, Tony had continued with extra enthusiasm. "Ever since, the strange cabin's been haunted. Folks say that Trapper John's ghost stays at the shack, tryin' to keep people away on account of the mad bear. And, as far as I know, nobody's ever stayed there all night. The ghost drives 'em out."

Frankie's slim face had remained as motionless as stone. "Hell, you guys don't know what fear is until you been runnin' and hidin' from cops in empty houses, alleys, and boneyards. Now that's scary!"

Alone at the remote cabin, Frankie unsaddled his horse and tethered it in a little meadow so it could fill up on fresh feed. Gathering his gear, he entered the shack and scanned the dark interior. "Hell, this place don't look bad at all. I been in a lot worse dumps than this. Guess I'll roll out my bag near the fireplace and check out this place 'fore dark."

He scouted the old building in the waning light. Near the rusted cook stove, he squinted at the wall. "Some junk hangin' there. Would they be traps? Naw. This ain't that old trapper's cabin. This here's a cow camp."

As complete darkness fell, Frankie removed his boots and

slipped into his sleeping bag. Feeling tired from the long ride, he lay awake for some time, listening and wondering at the strange, dead silence of the forest. "Hell, there ain't even a cricket in this country," he thought, and he drifted into a light, nervous sleep.

Thump! Thump! Thump!

The racket snapped Frankie into a sitting position. Clutching the inside of his sleeping bag, he searched the darkness of the weathered cabin with wide eyes.

"What was that? Somebody knocking?" He reached for his flashlight and, staying in his bag, he slid against the fireplace wall. "What's wrong with this cussed light? It won't come on!"

Thump! Thump! Thump!

"What the hell? Whatever is that? Somebody's up there! And I've got no light!"

The black haired youth pulled his knees under his chin and stared in the direction of the loft. His mouth turned dry as he tried to block out the tale of Trapper John and the mad bear.

"A bunch of crap," he thought. "Ain't no such things as ghosts. And nothin's gonna run me outa here!" His fears eased as the scrapings and thumpings subsided.

Moments later, he clutched his bag and gaped into the darkness as new, louder rackets came from the loft.

"Somethin's comin' down! Through the trap door! Is it opening? Whatever is it?"

Frankie's imagination reeled as the hoots of a horned owl echoed through the woods. No longer could he suppress the strange story of Trapper John. Et by a bear! Boots and blood! His ghost lives in the cabin! And runs everybody off!

Wondering and trembling, Frankie flinched at a disturbance on the mantle above his head. "Jesus, it's gettin' close!" He grabbed a boot and flung it at the sound. As the shoe bounced onto the floor, the racket ceased and the cabin was quiet for a while.

Fearful of more commotion so close to him, he stayed in his bag and slid along the cabin wall to a corner. Huddling against the logs, he detected a new sound outside the building. "Somethin's pushin' against the walls! Breathin' heavy! Tryin' to get in! It must be a bear! I'm done for!"

A resonant growl spilled into the June night, sending Frankie into more puzzled, cold tremblings. "It is the bear! Where can I go? The loft? No! Outside? No! Jesus, I dunno!"

The rubbing ceased and the heavy footsteps faded into the night. "He's gone! But he might come back! What then?"

Remaining in his bag, the boy hunched into the corner, pressing his back against the walls and hugging his knees with his arms. He remained there through the night, worrying and wondering, as the strange noises came and went. Several times he thought of fleeing, only to stop at the sound of rubbing and heavy steps outside.

Just before dawn, a calm settled into the cabin, and it became quiet as a tomb. "Well, whatever was here is gone," Frankie thought. "What a night! I'm whipped! But now, maybe I can get some sleep."

He sagged to the floor as the welcome daylight spread into the shack, and the songs of thrushes and warblers rang through the trees.

A loud banging brought Frankie to his feet. "Who the devil?" he mumbled as he kicked off his bag and unbarred the door. He glared at his cousins.

"You scum bags! You set me up in here for a night of hell! This place is the pits! Spooks inside! Bear outside! Hey, I owe you for this!"

Not anxious to challenge Frankie's wrath, Marie and Isaac hesitated and stood at the doorway.

"Well, yeah, Frankie, we put you in here to see how tough you was. And you made it! That makes you really tough! 'Cause nobody's ever done it. 'Cept maybe Marie. She holed up here for part of a night when it was stormin'."

Frankie's anger remained. "But I still owe you! And you're gonna get it!" Scowling, he moved into the mid morning sun outside the cabin. "So you stayed here, huh, Marie? Tell me, d'you ever get a look at this spook? Or see the bear?"

Marie glanced at Frankie, then at the dark green fir trees beyond the cabin. "Yeah, I saw the spooks alright," she said to herself. "But should I tell him that the ghost was just a bunch of noisy packrats? And that the bear was an old Hereford bull? No, it's best I keep it a secret."

Out loud, she said, "Naw. Never did get a look at 'em. Couldn't see 'em in the dark."

CHAPTER XIV

POSSUM CHARLIE

On the first morning of trapping season, a small crowd gathered at the county fair grounds in Foxboro. Men of all ages, women, and boys visited in the cold damp air, waiting to take part in the first trapping derby ever held in DeWitt County. As trappers formed a line to register, expediters scurried between tents shouting last minute instructions.

The rules called for five sets per trapper, using lure and bait only, with no traps in dens, runs, or trails. Two judges would accompany each trapper to inspect the sets. The derby would settle, for a time, who could catch the biggest coon, possum, or fox on opening day.

By nine o'clock, the gathering had dwindled as contestants finished registering and began moving to the field with the judges.

In the registration tent, Maggie Doran stood, stretched, and looked at her watch. "Well, Mary Lou Bratton, it looks like we're done signing them up. Didn't take us long to run 'em."

The full faced, graying woman poured herself a cup of coffee and stepped outside. "Whoops! We got one more, Mary Lou. Oh, my! It looks like Old Possum Charlie! Lordy, Lordy! He'll stink up this tent and everything in it! Including you and me!"

The stooped, ageless man entered the tent and removed his grease soaked cap, letting his yellow stained, white hair flop onto his collar. Shuffling to the table in bib overalls as greasy as his cap, he grasped a pencil with long, crusty fingers and filled a registration card. "How much, ma'am?"

With her fingernails, Maggie took the card by the very edge, inhaling all the while through clenched teeth. "That'll be twenty-five dollars, Charlie. And here's the rules. You'll find the judges by the red pickup."

Following Charlie out the door, Mary Lou opened the other

tent flap, her large bottom bouncing in skin tight jeans. She whispered to Maggie. "Whew! Do you suppose he's ever had a bath? I'll bet he hasn't changed clothes for years!" She shuddered as she tried to freshen the air in the tent by waiving her arms.

By noon, all of the trappers had been checked by the judges, all except Possum Charlie, who was still awaiting his turn.

Wondering, derby master Billy Don Hostetter approached the old man. "Whose your judges, Possum?"

"Don't know, Mistah Hostettah. They didn't tell me."

"Well, hang on. We'll find you some real quick."

Noticing Maggie and Mary Lou preparing to leave for lunch, the heavy set, silver haired derby master trotted toward the ladies. "Hey, gals, I've got a problem. Possum Charlie needs a couple of judges and there's none here."

Maggie glowered. "So?"

Billy Don forced a super smile as he looked over the tops of his glasses. "How 'bout you two goin' with Charlie and checkin' his sets? I'd be forever grateful."

The ladies grumbled, stomped, and scowled. "No way! We'd have to throw away our clothes after ridin' with him!"

The derby master looked away for a moment as he thought. "Tell you what, ladies. You can take my pickup and follow 'im. Today and tomorrow. And I'll see that you get some extra tickets for the drawing."

With faces mean enough to bite the heads off snakes, Maggie and Mary Lou glared at Billy Don. Their eyes bored into Billy Don's and forced him to look aside.

After several moments of dead silence, the derby master cleared his throat. "C'mon, ladies, give me a hand. Wha'dya say?"

The women looked at each other, and Mary Lou opened her hand. "Oh, alright, Mr. Derby Master. Let's have the keys. Just as well get it over with."

As the women left with Possum, Billy Don relaxed in the registration tent, sipping lukewarm coffee. "Got to admire those gals," he thought. "They're super. Yeah, Charlie smells. Hasn't washed for years. Not since his wife and little girls died from typhoid. Lived alone ever since.

"I'd be willin' to bet Old Charlie brings in a big coon. Or possum. Nobody knows 'em better."

On Sunday morning, a cold, light drizzle fell on the trappers as they checked their sets and brought their catches to the long white tent. Inside, the judges weighed, measured, and recorded the entries.

Billy Don stood inside the door of the judging tent, waiting for Maggie, Mary Lou, and Possum Charlie. He fidgeted throughout the morning, mumbling and wondering. "Where in the world are those folks anyway? It's high time they were here."

He drifted to the rear of the tent for more coffee when one of the judges called. "Here they are, Billy Don."

Hurrying to the front, the derby master observed Mary Lou and Maggie coming his way, and Possum shuffling toward the judges. "What tha'?" he thought. "Charlie looks strange. And where is his cap? Oh, he's got a big coon. A giant.

"But the ladies. They're smilin'. Somethin's screwy here! They were madder than wet hens this morning!

"Hi, Mary Lou, Maggie. How'd it go?"

Their smiles broadened as rain dripped from their noses. "Great! Best mornin' ever."

Billy Don stared at the ladies over the tops of his specs, puzzled and wondering. "C'mon, now, what's so great about it? The rain?"

"Nope."

"Charlie's big coon?"

"Nope."

"What then?"

Mary Lou and Maggie chuckled. "Old Possum got his first bath in twenty years!"

"Bath? How?"

"Well, he fell in Deep Creek and we took our time fetchin' him out!"

CHAPTER XV

IN THE CITY

Near the edge of her garden in Cherry Creek, spinster Elouise Higgenbotham was whimpering and fretting worse than a motherless pup. "Why, whatever happened to my Chinese poplar? It's gone! Nothing but a mutilated stump and chips. Some ill-mannered brat must have hacked it down and carried it away." The large bun of white hair on top her head quivered and her eyes glared as she stomped toward the house in the cool October air. "I'm going to get to the bottom of this. Perhaps Alonzo Lara would know if any hoodlums have been hanging around here."

Finding the part-time gardener next door, Elouise led him to the stump. "There, Alonzo, isn't that the work of vandals?"

Alonzo kept his voice on a mellow key. "Well, ma'am, this wasn't done by kids. A beaver cut your tree and drug it off."

Elouise blinked her eyes in rhythm with her quivering lip. "Beaver? Why, where did it come from? And why did it take my tree?"

The tall, high cheek-boned caretaker continued his smooth diplomacy. "You see, ma'am, wherever there's a creek or ditch or water, there's liable to be beaver. This 'un here prob'ly come outa that ditch over there lookin' for somethin' to eat."

"Eat? Do beaver eat garden trees?"

"Yes'm. They'll eat the bark of almost any hardwood."

The elderly socialite studied the stump and Alonzo's unmoved face. "Do you suppose, Alonzo, that the beaver will destroy more of my trees?"

"Yes'm, prob'ly will. Because there's gettin' to be so many beaver that they're desperate for food. They're chewin' on trees all over town."

"But what will I do? I just can't lose my precious trees. There must be some way to stop them."

Alonzo scraped some phlegm from his throat and waited a moment to reply. "Well, Miss Higgenbotham, it's a tough problem. The only sure way I know of is, ah, well . . ." He hesitated to bolster his courage. "I mean, ma'am, you have to kill 'em, shoot 'em, or trap 'em."

Elouise tightened her withered lips and turned the powdery skin around her mouth into a thousand fine wrinkles. "Kill them? Oh, my no. That's barbaric! Surely there's a humane way to stop them."

Alonzo paused and surveyed other golden leafed trees near the edge of the garden. "I've heard that the city hired some experts to tell 'em how to control beaver. Not sure what they came up with but you could call 'em and find out."

"Humph. I don't know about calling the city bureaucrats. Do they really know anything? I believe I'll wait and see. Perhaps the beaver won't come back."

During the following week, however, Elouise lost another poplar and a maple to the raiding beaver. She learned that her neighbor, tiny Mme. Marie LeRoux, also lost several ornamentals.

Working herself into a dry froth, she hurried to Marie's giant front door and rang. "That's it, Marie! We must call the animal control people immediately. This has gone far enough. May I use your phone?"

"Please do, my dear."

With a quavering voice, Elouise told of beaver destroying her trees and asked what could be done.

"Yes, the city folks were aware of beaver cutting citizens' trees. Yes, the city had hired consultants to study and recommend courses of action. Yes, that's correct, beaver cannot be trapped. What do we recommend? Feed the beaver. And if that doesn't work, do what? Sterilize them? But how? Oh, my goodness!"

Elouise slammed the ornate gold phone into its holder. Her dry floury skin flushed pink and her brow furrowed. "Oh, my. I can't believe it. What vile talk! Why that man should be discharged!"

"What is it, Elouise? What did he say?"

"I can't repeat it! It's simply revolting. Filthy! Obscene!"

Mme. LeRoux placed her slender hand on Elouise's shoulder. "Now, Louise, darling, surely not all of his conversation was obscene. Didn't he say anything worthwhile?"

Elouise hung her head for several moments, then looked into the wide hallway as Alonzo entered. "Well, yes, Marie, he did say that we could try feeding them with fresh cut limbs."

Mme. LeRoux studied Alonzo's face. "Would feeding the beavers work, Alonzo?"

The caretaker forced a courteous smile. "Not likely, ma'am. I've never heard of it."

Elouise remained tense. "Well, we have to try something. Alonzo, see if you can find some branches and place them wherever you think best. You know about beaver."

After numerous calls, the caretaker located some fresh cottonwood cuttings at one of the city dumps and placed them in the beaver's path. For the next two weeks, he checked the limbs every morning but found none missing. In Mme.'s yard, however, two more trees had been cut by the beaver.

Wondering, tiny Marie summoned Alonzo and they called on Elouise. "Louise, my dear, the feeding isn't working. The animals are still biting off our trees. Tell me, what other method did the city personnel mention? Did you say sterilization?"

Elouise blinked and twitched. "Oh, my, I can't repeat it!"

"Really, Louise, what was their suggestion?"

The spinster shot her eyes at Marie then at Alonzo, and back at Mme. LeRoux. "Oh, it's foul, Marie. Horrible! He said, he mentioned, that we would have to castrate the males! Oh, there, I said it! Have mercy!"

She sank onto the love seat and buried her face in her hands.

Mme. LeRoux suppressed a smile. "Well, I must say this sounds like a very unusual procedure. Do you think, Alonzo, that beaver could be sterilized?"

Stroking his square chin, the gardener blinked his eyes as he talked. "No ma'am, I wouldn't know how. There's no way I know of that would sterilize all the male beavers. In fact, I don't know how you could sterilize even one in the wild."

"Why is that, Alonzo?"

"Well, ma'am, you'd have to catch 'em first. And since trapping isn't allowed, there's no way to get a hold of 'em."

Marie turned to Elouise. "But surely there must be some reasonable way. Or why would they recommend it?"

Elouise rose as her face continued to tremble. "Well, I most assuredly don't know. But I do know, I'm calling the mayor. He will tell me or else!"

She stomped to the phone and dialed with a shaking finger.

"The mayor's not available? But I must speak with him about these beaver. Not 'til next week? Well, alright, connect me with Animal Control."

Her lower lip twitched out of control. "Yes, I've tried feeding. It doesn't work. But what I need to know is this, this sterilizing. How should I go about it?"

The spinster put her hand over the mouth piece. "He's calling a visiting biologist to the phone." Her face relaxed as she waited for the expert's words.

"Find a what? With a what?" She returned the phone to the table and pressed her frail hands against the sides of her face. "Alonzo, that man, that biologist, he said that, to sterilize beaver, I should find a scuba diver with a fast knife.

"Now what on earth did he mean by that?"

Alonzo glanced at Marie and Elouise, then stared into the

yard through the French window. "Sounds like he's wantin' to be funny. Makin' a joke, an impossible joke. No way could the city 'crats sterilize all the beaver in Denver. And what good would it do? Sterilized beaver are still gonna eat. And new beaver are gonna be movin' in.

"What we need is a trapper, an animal control person that does just that. Like in the Netherlands. Every village has a trapper that controls muskrats year 'round. Yeah, they kill thousands of muskrats. They have to. If they didn't, their dykes would be riddled with holes and borrows and the dykes would wash away."

Elouise held her forehead with an unsteady hand. "Alonzo, isn't there anything I can do?"

The caretaker drew a deep breath and paused a moment. "Well, ma'am, none that I know of. You're just stuck with marauding beavers. And it's gonna stay that way until we put some intelligent people in city hall. It's hopeless."

CHAPTER XVI

THE LION HUNTERS

In late February, 1923, a violent blizzard pummeled the lion hunters' cabin near Wolf Creek in Glacier National Park. The storm, beginning its third day, whipped the snow into a blinding wall of white and shot it through the forest with merciless fury.

Inside the tiny cabin, Reno Johansen, a heavy set young Swede, mumbled to himself as he spooned sourdough batter onto a smoking griddle. "Damn. Stuck in this shack for another day. Ain't this storm gonna end? And cookin'. I hate it. Same old crap, dry corn bread, tough cakes, mouldy bacon. And eggs that make you gag. Here, Ugly, your breakfast."

With a bent fork in his hand, Jaque Roulier glared at the Swede. "Ain't there no more syrup than this?" He shook the empty can over the cakes. "These goddamn boards need at least a quart so's you can get a fork in 'em."

The red on Reno's face deepened. "There ain't no more. 'Cause you been hoggin' it all winter. If you don't like these cakes, fix yer own."

The Frenchman's upper lip curled. "Jesus. Your cookin's getting about as rotten as your disposition. Gimme a couple of them month old eggs."

Reno's torso quivered. "Here's your eggs, bastard!" He lifted a hard fried egg and winged it into Jaque's face and followed with another that stuck in Jaque's long black hair.

With a snarling oath, Jaque leaped at Reno, flailing his fists in wide circles. Losing his balance he crashed into Reno, and they fell to the floor, pulling hair and beards, and hissing like mad cats. They tumbled into the small table, scattering utensils, batter, and condiments onto the floor and sending the terrified red bone hound under the bottom bunk.

Punching and kicking, the pair rolled into the bunk, across the room, and on top the ropes and snares. There they collapsed from exhaustion, and lay on the floor, chests heaving and anger

89

vented. The Swede rolled to his side, rose, and limped toward the door, feeling a new lump above his eye. "Gotta cool off. These walls are gettin' too close."

After a short stay in the refreshing power of the wind, Reno entered the cabin and spoke in a low shaky voice. "Jaque, we gotta get apart for a few days. 'Fore we kill each other. Besides, we ain't seen a lion track for over a week. And we're needin' some fresh grub. Specially the dogs. The corn bread ain't cuttin' it. Why don't we take off a few days and then go to the head of Bowman Lake, where the Park Rangers said that big old male cat hangs out."

The older, slender lion hunter looked wild as a long haired baboon, with red eyes peering through the crumpled black hair and beard. "Yeah, you're right. Get to town for a few days. On the way back, we can stay at Lake MacDonald for a night, then go on to Bowman. The rangers said we could stay at their summer cabin there." His words turned into a soft whisper. "I want to see Jewel. I need to see her real bad."

Reno's eyes drifted toward the small window and he stared at the storm. "Jewel" he thought. "Best lookin' dame in Kalispell. Hmph." A tiny grin eased his stressed face. "You sure she'll be waitin? Must be a dozen guys hangin' 'round her."

"Don't you worry none, Johansen. Jewel is mine and I know she is true. We'll be gettin' married one of these days. Soon as I can find somethin' better than ketchin' cats alive."

Reno stepped closer to the dingy glass to size up the incessant wind. "Oh, yeah, how does he know what she's doin' when he's up here? Oh, well, that's none of my business."

Just before dawn on the following morning, Jaque and Reno loaded their packboards, gathered the four hounds, and started the long trek to Polebridge. In the silent, quiet, deadly cold, they trudged with slow deliberate steps, for their snowshoes were sinking four to six inches in the new snow. With numb finger tips and trembling bodies, they yearned for the rising sun to ease the biting cold.

At noon, they stopped at a protected opening in the spruce forest and ate some dry cornbread and cold beans. Jaque fed the dogs chunks of dry cake for their strength and vigor had ebbed. As the men swallowed their last bites, they moved onto the trail without resting.

Jaque snorted through the white frost on his beard and moustache. "Goddamn, it's cold. That sun don't help much. I'll sure be glad to reach Lake MacDonald and warm up in the engineer's cabin. Ahh, I can feel the heat already."

Reno coughed and spit a gob of yellow flem into the snow. "Yeah, the only heat you can feel is your fingers turning to ice inside your gloves."

Ignoring the remark, Jaque hummed an improvised tune over

and over as he shuffled through the snow. "Waltzing Jewel, Waltzing Jewel, you'll come awaltzing, my Jewel with me."

Nearing the junction of Wolf Creek and the south tributary of Lake MacDonald in late afternoon, the two slabbed across a steep, shaded hillside. In this dense stand of spruce, they felt the cold sink into their bones and they labored to quicken their steps.

On the far edge of the thicket, the red bone hound gave a yelp. Blue and the others also bayed and they tugged at their leashes to follow the giant track.

Jaque stared at the sign with blinking eyes. "It's him! That old male. What a paw!" He hung his head. "But we can't take after him today. There's only an hour of daylight left, and no way we can spend the night in this cold. Damn the luck!"

Reno slid to the side of the trail where the dogs hadn't scattered the track. "Whooee! What a paw! But you're right, we can't chase him today. Maybe we can figger a way to get him later. On the way back."

For a few moments, as Reno studied the prints and the anxious dogs, Jaque slid his snowshoes onto the trail. "Better get movin'. Still got a long ways to go." And he hummed another tune about Jewel.

An hour after sunset, Jaque and Reno shuffled up the steps of the engineer's cabin. Jaque trembled as he searched for signs of life. "What th'? Charlie's gone! Now ain't that a stab in the crotch! But just where the devil are we gonna stay tonight? We don't dare break into this place."

Reno pointed to a boat house in the ghostly light of a half moon. "How about that shack? Must have a stove, 'cause there's a pipe stickin' out the roof."

The pair entered the open boat house and searched the darkness for signs of a stove. Reno squinted into the darkness. "My god, look at the cracks in the walls. Must be a good half inch between the boards. This place is gonna be cold. Damn cold."

Reno fished a candle from his pack, and lighting it, he discovered a stove. "Jesus, this midget wouldn't melt bacon grease if'n it was red hot. Guess I'd better russle up some wood. Lots of it."

Through the long night of 40 below, the pair took turns shoving scrap wood into the tiny stove. Both men and dogs shivered, barely avoiding freezing and wishing for daylight and its warming sun.

Leaving ropes, snowshoes, and other supplies in the boat house, Reno and Jaque shouldered their packboards again before dawn and left with shivering hounds. They walked with ease along the packed trail, reaching the livery at Polebridge late in the afternoon.

The Frenchman slapped the wrangler on his dusty back.

"Hey, Dale, how about taking care of these mutts for a few days? They need some meat. And we'll be back in four days. Right now we need some hot grub."

The slow moving livery operator narrowed his eyes at the dogs. "Yeah, I guess so. But I don't like 'em. All they do is howl. Nothin' but trouble."

At the tiny Grubstake Cafe, Jaque wiped some stew gravy from his plate with fresh bread. "Okay, Reno, I'll see you here in four days. You gather up enough grub and supplies for another week or so. I'm goin' to Kalispell to see my Jewel."

Reno turned his eyes to the side. "Might wander over to Kalispell myself. One night at least."

Jaque's red lips showed through his beard as he laughed. "Hell, you're gonna go down and get drunk, and end up in the cat house." He grasped his friend's shoulder and squeezed. "Don't take much money down there. You might get rolled."

After dinner, the pair separated, with Reno staying with his trapping friend Eric Nelson and Jaque hopping the evening train to Kalispell.

Late the next day, Reno, having satisfied his appetite with fresh food, grabbed his friend Eric and they, too, boarded the train for Kalispell.

After two days in the town, Reno returned to Polebridge and gathered his food and supplies. On the morning that they were to depart, he stomped and fidgeted outside the livery stable. "Now what's keepin' that lady killin' Frenchman? We gotta get movin'. The sun's high already."

Within an hour, Jaque skipped into the livery with steps as light as a spider. "Hey, Reno, did I ever have a blast with Jewel! What a doll!"

Reno's agitated face intensified. "You're late. C'mon, we gotta get goin'." He swung his pack onto his back and gathered the dogs. "So did your Jewel put you up at night?"

"Now look here, Reno. She ain't that kind. I stayed at a hotel. Course I didn't see her much except in the mornings, her working so late in that bar."

Reno gave no reply, nor did he make much conversation on the way to Polebridge. His eyes were distant and preoccupied, and his mind oblivious to Jaque's elated chatter about his lady friend.

They walked into Lake MacDonald well after dark, and finding Charlie Biorgen at home, they spent a comfortable night.

Jaque pressured the dejected Reno to converse, but the young trapper offered very few words. The Frenchman forced a laugh. "And did you hear about that big lion we shipped to El Paso? Damn thing broke out of his crate and was running around town. Scared the devil outa the folks. And the cops had to shoot it 'cause they couldn't catch it."

Charlie chuckled at the story while he stuffed more wood into the iron stove. "Well, one thing for sure, those cats are dangerous, and you boys had better be careful. If one landed on your back, you'd get tore up bad."

At daybreak the next morning, the hunters loaded their packs and headed for the Ranger's summer cabin at Bowman Lake. They hiked with ease for a chinook wind had melted much of the snow and the air was warm. Still quiet and spiritless, Reno followed Jaque, head down and ignoring the dogs.

Arriving at the Bowman Lake cabin, they unloaded their heavy packs and built a fire. As Jaque fed the dogs, he gazed at Reno, then at the floor. "Dunno what's eatin' Reno. He's usually purty gassy after a stay in town. Musta got drunk. Real drunk. And maybe he's still hung over."

Reno squinted at the frozen lake as he went outside for wood. "What will I say," he pondered. "Maybe nothin'. Keep my mouth shut. But he oughta know. He's my friend. Lord, I dunno."

"Hell, I gotta do it."

After their dinner of thick venison stew, Reno cleared the table except for a mug of sour coffee. "Jaque, I gotta tell you somethin'. I seen your girlfriend in Kalispell."

"Yeah? Where? At Jonsey's Bar?"

"Nope. Down on Emporium."

"What was she doin' there?"

"Workin'. Late."

"Hell, she don't work down there."

Reno bent close to Jaque, his eyes piercing his friend's.

"Oh, yeah, she does. Me and Eric Nelson seen her. Upstairs in Ethel's Whorehouse. For five bucks a throw, just like the rest of the girls."

CHAPTER XVII

CAN TRAPPERS READ?

In late September, Gunnison elementary school principal Derwin Appleby sat quiet as a manikin in his green high backed chair. Flanked by seven members of his staff, the principal fixed his gaze on Chris Sloan, a short, stocky graying man seated at the end of the conference table. "What gall," Appleby thought, "wanting to take his handicapped son Eddy out of school. This man's an illiterate, a wood rat. Look at him, unshaven, mouth full of sneuss, high water jeans smelling of oil. Why must I waste my time on this low life, this trapper? He can't understand, just gets unruly, threatening."

The headmaster rested his elbows on the table and folded his hands. "Now Mr. Sloan, as you have heard here today, your son is dyslexic and needs intensive instruction such as we provide here. There is no way you could teach him at home. He must be taught by our skilled professionals."

With a flick of his tongue, Chris pushed the wad of Copenhagen to the bottom of his gum. "Just one thing, Mr. Appleby. Eddy's been in your Special Ed deal for four years. And he ain't learned squat. Nothin'. Your teachers don't teach him anything. They just babysit. And I'm sick of it."

Trembling, he shoved another gob of tobacco under his lip. "I'm gonna take him outa this school and teach him at home. Me and my wife. I know damn well he'll learn more there than here. This place is a joke."

"I knew it! Obnoxious, threatening," thought Appleby. Hiding his anger, he swelled with power. "Let me warn you, Mr. Sloan. You cannot remove your child from school and teach him at home unless you or your wife are certified teachers. And you are not, are you? Why, you can't even read, can you, Mr. Sloan?"

Chris' face grew crimson under the pepper colored, two day beard. He spoke with a low, quavering voice. "I know I'm not

educated like you people here, 'cause I've spent most of my life
in the woods, loggin' and trappin'. But I can teach my boy. Hell,
he already knows more about the outside than any of you in here
will ever know."

He rose, shoved the chair against the table, and stomped
from the room.

In the month that followed, Chris Sloan kept his son at
home. When he went to the woods to log, he showed Eddy how
to lop small branches and perform other simple chores, and they
both travelled together on the trapline. In the evenings, he and
his wife Janet struggled trying to teach Eddy the alphabet.

Exactly thirty days from the meeting with Appleby, Chris
recieved a certified letter from the school. He snorted as Janet
read the notice in the tiny kitchen of their aging log home.
"Those bastards, gonna take me to court if I don't put Eddy back
in school. Just 'cause we ain't qualified teachers. I oughta go
down and stack 'em in a corner."

His wife placed her reddened hand on his shoulder. "Now,
Christopher, you can't do that. You'll just get in real trouble.
These people call themselves educators, but sometimes they act
like cops. Do what they want. They have lots of power."

Her round, soft face brightened. "Tell you what, though, go
down and tell them we are getting a qualified teacher."

Chris's eyes widened. "We are? Really? Who?"

"Now I been talking to Polly Donnigan, the optometrist's
widow. She taught school years ago, you know. And she said she
might be able to help Eddy."

With eyes still wide, Chris scooped out the lump of spent
sneuss from his lip. "Now that sounds great! And they won't be
able to haul us to court. I'm gonna run down there tomorrow and
give Appleby the good news."

At nine the following morning, Chris donned clean pants and
shirt and made his way to the school receptionist's desk. His jaw
was set, and his cheeks pulsated with each grind of his teeth.
"Wanna see Appleby. About this letter." He shot the paper onto
the desk.

Remaining cool and trying to look pleasant, the clerk
returned the letter. "I'm sorry, Mr. Appleby is in a meeting and
won't be available until tomorrow. Could you come back then?"

Chris continued to grind his teeth. "Tomorrow, huh? What
time?"

The receptionist scanned her desk calendar. "How about
eleven?"

"Yeah, okay, eleven. I'll be here." He trudged out the hall
and climbed into his faded blue pickup. "Rats, another day
wasted. But there's nothin' I can do."

At eleven fifteen the next morning, Chris entered the
hallowed hall of principal Appleby, who was seated behind a

huge desk and joined by the spectacled psychiatrist and an older, bearded man. "Damn, they got me outnumbered again," he thought. "They must be like sheep. Great strength in numbers."

"Good morning Mr. Sloan. Do sit down. You remember Mr. Ackman, our psychiatrist. And this is our school attorney Mr. Weisberger.

"I assume you have received my letter instructing you to return your son to school or face court proceedings. May I remind you that it is unlawful to take your child out of school without providing a certified teacher to instruct him."

"Yeah. You told me that before. But how come there's some other kids learnin' at home, like the three McGraw boys? How come they're not in court?"

Appleby looked at Sloan with a merciless glare. "That's simple. Mrs. McGraw was an elementary school teacher for several years. Now, may we expect Eddy to be in school tomorrow?"

Chris's eyes fell, then lifted to meet Appleby's. "Bull. McGraws get away with it 'cause they got money. We're keepin' Eddy at home 'cause we have a lady lined up to tutor him. Gonna start next week. She lives just a block away."

Appleby felt his control slip. "But, Mr. Sloan, we will have to examine this person's credentials to determine that she is qualified. You just can't choose any lay person to teach your child. That's absurd."

"Yeah, well this lady is a good teacher, that I know. And I'm not bringin' Eddy back for you to babysit."

Chris stood, and forcing a smile, gave the trio a view of his tobacco stained teeth. "Hasta luego," and he banged his heels on the floor as he left the room.

Remaining in the executive suite, the officials discussed their next move. Mr. Appleby pressed his point. "We must require Mr. Sloan to produce credentials for the tutor. For all we know, he may have engaged another of his kind, some backwoods idiot. I think he should present the information by the end of next week. Does that sound reasonable, Gentlemen?"

Attorney Weisberger cleared his throat. "Reasonable, Derwin, very reasonable. We should avoid court if at all possible, for this kind of case is never cut and dried."

"Alright, then. We will issue a demand for the lady's qualifications. If they are not acceptable, we will follow the legal alternative."

As expected and dreaded, the Sloans received another certified letter from the school. Janet Sloan explained the utlimatum to Chris as she covered a bowl of bread dough. "Seems like they want to interview Mrs. Donnigan. So they can approve or disapprove. They want all three of us to meet them on Friday at ten."

For a few seconds, Chris squinted and blinked his blue eyes. "Not another trip to that office! All they do is have meetings. Just wrecks my work."

On Friday, the principal's conference room bulged once more with school officials, the director of special ed, two special ed teachers, the psychiatrist, the school nurse, the secretary, the superintendent, and Mr. Appleby. As Mrs. Donnigan and the Sloans found chairs, Chris mumbled to himself. "Outnumbered again. How can you beat these odds?"

After introductions, thin Polly Donnigan spoke in a soft voice. "I was raised on a farm in central Kansas. Life was rigorous and we had no luxuries. But I managed to enroll at State College and obtain a teaching certificate. Then I moved to western Kansas and taught grades one through six in a one room school. I taught there for seven years."

Appleby interrupted. "But, Mrs. Donnigan, you never received a degree. Is that correct?"

"That's correct, Mr. Appleby, no degree, because none was required for elementary school teachers at that time."

Reveling in power, Appleby continued his cross examination. "But what skills, Mrs. Donnigan, do you possess that makes you capable of teaching a severely handicapped boy like Eddy Sloan? Surely you must realize that this is a very difficult undertaking."

Polly Donnigan brushed her fingers against her white hair. "I realize that Eddy's problem will take much patience, but let me explain. My husband was an optometrist and he, like other optometrists, knew about kids with learning problems. These kids' eyes did not function properly, and, through the years, he gave some of the youngsters eye exercises along with other coordination drills. Soon they became winners instead of losers. I believe I can do the same for Eddy because I know these techniques well, and I know Eddy."

The school officials shifted in their chairs and snickered to themselves. Appleby's brow furrowed in puzzlement. "Mr. Grossman, what is your assessment of this, this eye therapy?"

The special ed director grabbed both lapels of his jacket and leaned against the back of his chair. "Well, there's been some baseless rumors about it, but there's nothing in the literature. It's strictly an unfounded claim by a few lay people. I don't know of any school that utilizes this technique."

Still standing, Polly looked around the table and made eye contact with each person. "I can assure you, folks, that these techniques do help. And if I can work with Eddy for two years, he will be able to read. Perhaps not fluently, but he will read."

Restless and seeking eye support from his colleagues, Appleby leaned on his elbows. "Well, Mrs. Donnigan, we are extremely doubtful about your proposal. And you do not hold a current teaching certificate."

Remembering that he had the power to crush, Appleby spoke like a judge. "So we will recess for ten minutes, Mrs. Donnigan and Mr. and Mrs. Sloan. You may be excused while we evaluate your proposal."

For a half hour, the Sloans and Polly waited in the hall while the power structure hacked at the proposed action. At last the doors opened and the parents and the tutor entered, their eyes searching the faces of school personnel for some indication of a verdict.

Appleby stood and with tight lips summarized the decision. "Against our better judgement, we are willing to allow this technique on a trial basis. We will require a progress report every three months. And, Mr. Sloan, this applies to this school year only. Do you understand?"

With a face softened with relief, Chris nodded. "Yeah, Mr. Appleby, we'll report back in December. We thank you for your consideration."

As the Sloans and Polly left, they thought they noticed a subtle trace of defeat on the faces of the school personnel.

Appleby whispered to himself. "Humph, I shall win in the long run. No hick from Kansas nor trapper from the backwoods can show us how to teach. Never."

Through the fall and winter, Polly put Eddy through eye exercises for an hour every morning. In addition, she worked him with a hanging ball, step routines, and the balance beam. As he began to master these movements, she added stress, little by little, and the boy developed some confidence.

As winter gave way to spring, Eddy's eyes moved smoothly, thus improving his sight and allowing him to begin reading simple books. His expression was bright and his head was high.

At the final evaluation of the school year, Polly Donnigan smiled softly as she had Eddy spell simple words while performing tricky physical routines.

"Now what do you folks think of Eddy's progress? Hasn't he improved considerably?"

The evaluators remained silent, so silent that Appleby was forced to break the quiet. "Yes, Mrs. Donnigan, we see a slight improvement. But this boy has a long way to go. He has many difficult hurdles to overcome. One extreme handicap is that he must live with a father who can't read and is of no help."

Polly's face remained warm, but her eyes penetrated Appleby's. "Regardless of his father, Eddy is reading. And as for believing that trappers and backwoods people can't read, just remember, I and my entire family trapped when I was young. And we all can read. Very well, in fact."

CHAPTER XVIII

EMILE

Near La Sauses by the Rio Grande,
Dwelt a farmer known as Emile Strand.

He labored day and night to clear the land,
Moving rocks by horse and brush by hand.

Farming was not to Emile's liking, though,
He favored trapping in wind, mud, and snow.

He brought home coyote, beaver, and the lowly rat,
Flopping them on the kitchen table by the cat.

In his kitchen, on a table soaked with blood and fat,
He skinned all his game, peering 'neath his oily hat.

Many a night as he worked his flashing knife,
He wondered why he had never won a wife.

A giant of a man, with rusty, kinky hair,
Emile socialized little with the ladies fair.

Reeking of musk and castor, his house was no winner,
Because it frightened off those who came to dinner.

But one day a lady immigrant took him by the arm
And fell in love with Emile and his brushy, stony farm.

Now the new wife was healthy, young, and stout.
She loved to clean and whisk the refuse out.

Within a week it seemed,
The entire house had gleamed.

Kitchen, pantry, hall,
These she polished all.

But with all that strain,
The musk did remain,

Seeping like a pall
Through roof, floor, and wall.

"Oh, dear, what will I do?" she cried,
"Soap, cleanser, pads, all I have tried.
"The odor is making me ill,
"It must go or I surely will!"

Soon autumn came and Emile laid his traps anew,
Dragging in beaver, large and small, and muskrats, too.

Inside the kitchen door, he lay them in a heap,
To 'wait a skinning while the hapless wife did weep.

"Come, now, my good Hilda, to skin the 'rats and beaver here,
"Is no different than dressing chickens from the rear.

"And to skin inside where it's warm and dry,
"Is cause to give thanks, not to whine and cry."

"But cry I cannot stop
"When I see that table top.

"My food is one complete disaster
"Tainted with that beaver castor.

"My garlic has no taste
"To use it is a waste.

"The coffee, too,
"Is like the stew,
"Tastes like boiled glue."

As fall into winter faded,
The sight of beaver she now hated.

Her face, once young and fair,
Was clouded with despair.

And in a sudden storm that did rage,
She flew out the door and crossed the sage.

Released now from that terrible cage
That seemed like an endless age.

"Poor woman, lost her mind,
"But no great loss, do I find.

"She simply could not see
"That best things do come free.

"Musk, the basis of perfume, we have ample.
"It costs less than any store bought sample."

Through the winter and the months to follow,
Emile's life was quiet and hollow.

But with the arrival of the summer fair,
Emile donned his best and brushed his wooly hair.

His rugged silhouette
Caught the eye of Paulette.

Slender, wistful, and shy,
She made all wonder why.

She would wink her blue eye
At one who could not cry.

Without delay she moved into the musky house,
Anxious and happy to be the farmer's spouse.

Though the smell of castor did remain,
Shy Paulette labored hard to refrain
From showing any signs of disdain.

For him, she strove hard to please,
Brewing beer and aging cheese,
Baking bread and pies, all of these.

But as nights of autumn lengthened,
The vapors of castor strengthened.

Yet Paulette's gentle face
Showed not a single trace
Of loathing the skinning race.

Onto the kitchen table more beaver came each day,
To replenish grease and castor as they lay.

To Emile, it didn't matter
Where she set his dinner platter.

"Now, my Paulette, have no fright
"That the table seems not right.

"What counts are the vittles here,
"The stew, the bread, cheese, and beer."

To him, the wife flashed a smile,
As her innards flinched the while.

These things must change, she thought,
To save what I have wrought.
Bit by bit, I will do all that I am able
To change forever that awful kitchen table.

So I must make him taste
Musk and fat in great haste.

For his sense of smell
Surely is not well.

A new approach I will take
In making stew, bread, and cake.

Into the pots of soup, without fail,
Will go bits of beaver fat and tail.

And butter for the bread
Will be a whole new spread.

Flavored with the musk of rat
Plus a little coyote fat.

He will think
That the stink
From the air
Spoiled his fare.

Then my spouse will surely know
Beaver from this house must go.

But of these deeds I must not tell,
Else I be killed and burned in hell.

Through the fall, Emile ate with great zest,

Chomping, swearing, "This grub is the best!"

As winter waned, neighbor Maggie Quinn stopped by,
To visit some, but more on the wife to spy.

Because the smell was so strong,
She wished not to stay too long.

Yet to lunch she agreed
To a strange tasting feed.

And her piercing eyes took in all
During the short time of her call.

Paulette in her timid way
Had not many words to say.

"Yes, Emile's great,
"Although of late
"His appetite
"Seems not quite right."

Smiling, the neighbor took her leave,
Satisfied with her sly retrieve
Of news that no one would believe.

As strong winds of March tore at the house,
Paulette fretted more about her spouse.

She had increased the vile potion
Through the winter, with the notion
That he would in one swift motion
Rid the house of that foul lotion.

And now at every meal, Emile's face grew white,
As he ate little from loss of appetite.

Now on one windy, fateful night
As he checked spring calves with oil light,
His neighbor Maggie Quinn made a call,
Who in that stormy dark told him all
Of things she thought she saw in the house,
And things she assumed were done by his spouse.

Stunned, Emile at once grew weak,
He choked, gasped, and could not speak.

He stared with crazed eyes

At the threatening skies.

"She says I have eaten beaver fat,
"Their scaly tails, and musk of rat.

"If her vicious words are true,
"What torment must I go through.

"Hearing lies of musk and cake,
"Although these, perhaps, I could shake."

He now clutched his throat with a trembling hand,
"But eggs fried in skunk fat I cannot stand!"

Barely breathing, he stumbled into the night,
Across the sage and forever out of sight.